Carole Hayman has bee[...]
speare Company, was o[...]
Joint Stock Theatre Com[...]
tion with the Royal Cou[...]
was until recently an Ass[...]

As well as her many awa[...] [...] [...] in theatre,
on television and the radio she also writes for television, her
most recent comedy series being co-written with Sue Town-
send, and called *The Refuge*. She lives in London.

CAROLE HAYMAN

All the best, Kim

Illustrated by Viv Quillin

GRAFTON BOOKS
A Division of the Collins Publishing Group

LONDON GLASGOW
TORONTO SYDNEY AUCKLAND

Grafton Books
A Division of the Collins Publishing Group
8 Grafton Street, London W1X 3LA

A Grafton Paperback Original 1988
Reprinted 1988

ISBN 0-586-07364-7

Printed and bound in Great Britain by
Collins, Glasgow

Set in Ehrhardt

To the North of England
(post-Election 1987)

'Lakeland',
Wordsworth Walk,
Off London Road.

MONDAY

Dear Nan,

Thank you for the birthday card, though I think I should mention that I am seventeen and not seven which was the number on it. I've used the £2 for some black nail varnish and a second-hand monkey wrench, which is great for getting at tricky nuts. Not that I have much use for it at the moment. I have written to six garages since I finished my Manpower Services course. Five did not reply and the sixth said they were closing down due to lack of custom. It's on a housing estate near Windscale.

Nan ... I've been wondering about coming down to London for a bit. There is nothing to do up here, and it's dead boring hanging round social services all day. The Job Centre personnel are sick of my face. Last time I went there the manager said compulsory National Service was the best he could suggest. When I pointed out that I am a girl, he said I could have fooled him and had I thought of applying to a travelling circus, they always had vacancies for performing cockatoos.

I know you and mam haven't seen eye to eye since dad died, but it honestly wasn't her fault. It was his own decision to take up off-shore drilling, she *told* him he had no head for heights. This is a chance to let bygones be bygones, so will it be alright for me to stay? I'm arriving on the three forty-five on Wednesday.

Love,
Kim.

62, Prison View,
Borough of Lambeth,
London.

Dear Mam,

Dead boring train journey. The buffet was closed due to
shortage of staff but I searched through all my zips and
found a half eaten Yorkie. Also, 18 bus tickets, the Swiss
army knife I thought I'd lost, some used chewing gum and
Dusty's toy mouse. The guard came by and told me to take
my feet off the seat. He said, 'Look at it this way, son, how
would you like it if your girlfriend had to sit there?' I
answered in a gruff voice so he wouldn't notice his mistake,
but I was a bit shocked at his ignorance. There must be
tons of girls who wear Doc Martins in London.

After Crewe it started to sleet so I did the Mirror
crossword (3 minutes) and had a snooze. I was looking
forward to the first view of London but I didn't see it. Just
rows and rows of dirty houses and now and then some
grey-looking grass. Nan was dead pleased to see me . . .
though a bit annoyed. She had kissed three total strangers
before recognizing me. We went by bus from the station to
her house. It took one hour twenty minutes. Twenty
minutes on the bus and an hour to wait for it to come.

We had liver and bacon for supper and watched
'Dynasty'. It is Nan's favourite at the moment and she
knows all the characters by name. She said I ought to get
some clothes like Krystle's and then I wouldn't have any
trouble getting a job. I said I'd feel daft and anyway how
could you do car maintenance dressed in a see-through
toga? She said I had a point.

I've got my old room. It seems much smaller and doesn't have a gas light any more. But the bed springs are the same and so is the eiderdown. I wish Dusty was curled up on it. I feel miles and miles away.

Write soon,

Kim, x

thursday

Dear Tracey,
          Arrived safely. No thanks to
British Rail, my compartment was
colder than a Bejam's freezer. Hope
you like the P.C.. I nicked it from me
nan's collection, she is mad on Princess Di.
Havn't seen a single junkie yet. A lad
did fall at me feet at Euston Station,
but it turned out he was taking a fit.
Have seen Buckingham Palace ...
well nearly ... there were some very
big Americans standing in front of me.
It is dead disappointing. It looks like
the corporation baths and wasn't got
a turret or out like that. Wrote 'Boy
George for Jesus' on the wall of
                    Westminster Abbey.
                              love
                              kim

Princess Diana admiring a
Venus Fly-Trap at the Chelsea
Flower Show.

❀

Tracey Marie Turbot

'Laburnums'

Crows Mere Crescent

off Lardan road

Printed in the E.E.C.

Dear Mam,

Went to sign on today. You should've seen the queue! It went right round the block and ended at the chippie. I'd had two small chips and a pickled egg by the time I got inside. The room was full of skinheads. They weren't bothering to queue, just standing around looking threatening and head-butting the walls.

The man at the Job Centre was very offhand until I mentioned I'd like to work in a garage and then he laughed loudly. He asked what training I'd had and when I said a YOPS course for acting he laughed even louder. He seemed to be in a bit of a state, but a lady from inside brought him a cup of tea and he calmed down after that. I explained that I'd heard things were better in the South but he just stared at his tea and stirred it round and round though I pointed out his sugar lumps were still in the saucer. He is obviously barking mad. In future I shall save the bus fare.

I haven't seen any rich people though Nan says there are plenty. I asked if she'd ever met one and she said only Princess Michael when she launched the Unisex Sauna, and Mrs Salmon on the day she won at Whist. Also my social life is a bit limited as I only know one female geriatric. Last night she asked me to walk her to Bingo. She's afraid of going by herself since Margery (Mrs Salmon) had her winnings snatched by a youth on roller-skates. She said no-one would come near if I was with her, I looked frightening enough to part the Red Sea. Bingo isn't my idea of a raving London occasion, but I did meet two girls standing in the street. One was waiting for her mam, she walks her there twice a week because she is aggro-something. The other is her friend who guards them with a lemon Jif. They are called Janice and Ruth.

11

I'll have to stop now as my second sheet of paper is otherwise employed. Nan has run out of bog roll again.

Bye for now,
Kim.

SATURDAY

Dear Tracey,

It has rained every day for a week. Can't go out as it makes me Mohican go all limp. What's happening with you? Are you still going out with Naff Nigel? Best looking thing I've seen down here was in the wax works at Madame Tussaud's. He was a mass murderer. Am totally skint and won't get a giro for another week. The dole office here is horrible. It smells of old clothes and pee. Serves them right for not providing a lavvy.

Nan's conversation would kill Einstein's brain cells. If she's not on about soccer thugs, it's the Royal family or the vicar being gay. Did meet two girls in the street the other day. They are my last hope of staying sane cooped up with an eighty-two-year-old loony with angina and corns!

Write and tell me what is going on!

Kim.

THURSDAY

Dear Mam,

Nan keeps asking me when I'm going to get a job. She doesn't seem to realize there aren't that many openings for girls in the car trade. She says Mrs Salmon's son Reg runs a garage and maybe he'd take me on as a petrol pump assistant. She's going to ask Mrs Salmon next time she goes to her lunch club.

12

Ruth and Janice came to call for me today. Ruth only lives up the road. She's got three brothers and two sisters and her parents are Jamaican. Janice lives on a housing estate. I asked her what it was like and she said great, now she's got used to the wind. They live on the twenty-ninth

floor. Her brother's got a motor bike. I asked if he'd let me have a go on it but she said he never takes it out on the road. He keeps it in the living room and cleans it every day. I like them 'cos they laugh at everything I say. I've never had an audience for my witty remarks before.

Nan was a bit shocked about Ruth. She said it was bad enough having me going around looking like a plague victim without inviting 'Blackies' into the house. I'm going

13

out with Ruth and Janice tomorrow night. They're taking me to a warehouse to hear a band called 'The Four Skins'.

Lots of love,
Kim.

P.S. Is Dusty pining for me?

Social Services

TUESDAY

Dear Mam,

Today I rang up for a job that was advertised in the South London News. Painter and decorator wanted. A woman answered the phone. She said thank you for calling, but they had to have a man. I said you're not allowed to say that, there's a law been passed against it. She got a bit flustered and said it wasn't that she didn't want a girl it was just that the work would be too heavy. I said I thought I could manage a paint tin, I could pick up my Nan with one arm. But she only giggled and said her husband's decision was final. I rang the equal opportunities commission but they were out. A grim looking man has just beckoned me to his grille . . .

Later.

I cannot get a special grant for new Doc Martins. But if I die of pneumonia from having wet feet you will get £10 to pay for my coffin.

Here's hoping,
Kim.

P.S. I have found out why Ruth and Janice laugh at everything I say. They think my accent is hilarious.

14

THURSDAY

Dear Tracey,

Saw some street theatre today. It is what out of work people do in London. It was on a pile of rubble where the council are building an adventure playground. It is quite adventurous already as the kids' favourite game is throwing bricks at each other. The actors sang, told jokes and ducked a lot. The audience consisted of me and a bag lady. After a while the bag lady got a mouth organ out and joined in.

At the end, one of the actors came round with a hat. I didn't have any money so I gave them two stamps and a stale ham sandwich I was going to give to the ducks. When he got to the bag lady she said 'god bless you, dearie', and took the hat and everything in it.

I talked to the actors afterwards. They were five blokes and a girl. The blokes explained that their art was devoted to exposing inequality. While they were chatting the girl did the clearing up and brought us a cup of tea. They asked me if I'd like to join. They pooled their giros and each took out what they needed. Later I heard the girl ask if she could have 5p to buy herself a fag, so I was glad I had said no. Anyway, I am still waiting for a giro.

Kim.

P.S. It's nothing much. I didn't move fast enough to miss a flying cooker.

SATURDAY

Dear Mam,

Yes, I did go to the warehouse with Ruth and Janice but I didn't mention it in my last letter as I didn't want to worry you.

Nan says I am not to invite Ruth round again. She says her family are squatters and it's not right 'darkies' having a house when decent people are still on the waiting list. She says 'darkies' never pay the rent and if she had her way they'd all be put out on the street. Either that or locked in their flats until they starve to death. I suggested to her that her views were a bit politically extreme, but she said she didn't hold with politics, she always voted Tory.

Yours in despair!
K.

P.S. Kattomeat is *41p* at the corner shop!

Bed.

WEDNESDAY

Dear Mam,

What do you mean what did I mean about 'worry' you? I didn't mean anything, it was just a slip of the pen. I don't think I'll be going there again though as Ruth has now been banned.

Ruth took me to visit Janice in the Tower. The lift was out of order so we had to walk up twenty-nine flights. Flippin' 'eck! Shows you how out of condition you are! There was a lot of writing on the walls and when we got to the tenth floor there was a pile of something nasty.

Janice's mum is very depressed, she takes pills all the time and keeps talking about doing herself in. She says with a laugh that she doesn't need no do it yourself leaflet on suicide, all she has to do is step out on to the balcony and there it is twenty-nine floors below. She said it twice while we were there, once when Janice's dad left for work and said he wouldn't be back 'til Friday and once when Janice's brother Errol called her a raasclaat cow because she wouldn't give him her housekeeping money to buy new handlebars for his bike. Errol has been on the dole for eighteen months but he keeps his bike dead nice. I have offered to lend him my monkey wrench if I can strip his carburettor.

Janice said she had to do the shopping as her mam can't get out much. We saw her dad go into the betting shop but Janice said not to say anything as he'd only turn nasty. He works on building sites and is often away for two or three weeks. She says it's a good thing as he and her mam don't get on that well and last time he was home she had to stop her mam jamming the bread knife in him when he was in a drunken coma. I asked her why she doesn't leave (she is nearly eighteen) but she said her mam really would kill herself if she did and she doesn't want that hanging over her for the rest of her life. She reckons she'll be married by the time she's twenty. Ruth hasn't got a boyfriend. She's on probation for doing GBH to her last one.

The weather has turned mild at last, Nan now takes her hat off in the house. We are going for a day out in Bognor. Nan says she hasn't had any sea air since a kipper went off in the larder.

Can you send me that picture of Dusty Auntie Madge took in the garden? There's a frame on the tallboy it would just fit into right.

Write soon,
Kim.

P.S. There's a wedding shot of you and dad in the frame. You're smiling which just goes to show you must have liked him once.

17

Dear Mam,

No of course I haven't been 'glue sniffing' or 'head banging'. Ruth didn't get banned for anything like that. If you
must know it was because she called the youth worker a
raasclaat. I am not sure what it means, but apparently he
didn't like it. It's not the first time she has had bother at
the club, it is also where she ~~bottled~~ had an argument with
her boyfriend. Anyway she doesn't like the youth worker,
he's white and he threatened to tell her probation officer
that she'd put a b. ~k through the window. She says white
people shouldn't mix in black culture, they cause all the
trouble. I think she is a 'separatist'.

Nan and I had a fab time at the seaside. We didn't go to
Bognor as the guard put us on the wrong train. Nan said it
was a sorry day for England when British rail got Home
rule. We went to Southend and I had my fortune told by
Feroza Petulengro on the pier. She said I had a colourful
future, Nan said she must have been looking at my hair.
She asked me to cross her palm with a fiver but I'd spent
up by then so she had to settle for one and two in old
money from the bottom of Nan's handbag and a picture of
Fergie that Nan cut out of Slimmer's Weekly. Nan and she
had quite a tussle over that. But Nan gave in when Feroza
threatened her with the gypsy's curse.

I have had to stay in the rest of the week as Nan had
four cups of tea, two ice creams and a go on the Waltzer
out of my giro, so I've mended the washing machine at last.
I had to use a wire hanger as a spare part as Nan's model
is obsolete. The last time it worked properly was 1933.

Write soon, thank Dusty for the paw print.
Kim.

P.S. I should have made it clear that Ruth only put the brick through the window because the ~~raasclaat~~ youth worker wouldn't let us in.

Lots of love, K.

Battersea Park.

Dear Mam,

Thanks for the money. It came in dead handy as I'd have been completely housebound without it . . . like you always used to say you were. I was getting on Nan's nerves hanging around all day. She kept saying it reminded her of when Grandad was alive.

Unfortunately I have spent it already. A fiver does not go far in London. We had fish and chips for our tea yesterday and Nan said she'd have to take out a mortgage to pay for them. The chip shops are rotten. They don't do mushy peas or curry sauce. Nan is disgusted by chips with curry sauce, she says we have been taken over with Common Market muck. She has now banned everything non-English from our diet, she went mad when I chucked the Irish cheddar, Dutch tomatoes and corned beef from Brazil.

Ruth's probation officer has got her on a scheme for painting murals. It's part of a plan for cheering up what he calls 'deprived' areas. Ruth says he means ghettoes. What you do is find a bit of waste land (like where houses have fallen down and the council haven't built any new ones) and if it's got a wall still standing, you paint on it. Ruth turned up the first day with her spray can and wrote 'PORNOGRAPHY IS VIOLENCE AGAINST WOMEN' on her bit, but the community worker said it wasn't direct enough, so she sprayed it out and wrote 'ALL MEN ARE

19

BASTARDS' instead. The community worker explained that what he meant by 'direct' was 'strikingly visual', so she painted a Cruise Missile with 'BIG DICK' written on the side. The community worker told her he'd have her taken off the project if she was going to cause trouble and to get on and spray up some trees and a cow.

Ruth's asked me if I'll go with her tomorrow. I've got nothing else to do. I wrote off for sixteen jobs last week and I haven't had a single reply. I know I am not really qualified to be a computing consultant or a research assistant in human geography, but I'm willing to learn.

Love,
Kim.

P.S. I have found out what raasclaat means. I won't go into details but don't use it in every day conversation.

The Public Library

Lou Goldenblatt,
Shilling Chambers,
Pound Street,
Bank.

Dear Sir or Madam,

I would be very interested in becoming a trainee broker. I am a bit younger than you want, but *am* hard working and presentable. My only experience of high finance is my post office savings account. Unfortunately there is nothing in it at the moment as I am out of work. There was two pounds forty pee until last week, but I moved it to my Nan's holiday club where you get a better return.

Yours sincerely,
Kim Kirby.

Dear Mam and Dusty,

I don't know why you've got this thing about Ruth, she's really great. Even Nan has come round now Ruth's told her she used to be in the guides. I've never met anyone like her. Social workers tremble when they go round to her house. She's not even scared of the SPG though they charged her brother Clovis with standing at a bus stop.

I went to help her on 'The Wall' as we call it. It is one side of a disused factory. This area is littered with them. We are doing a mural called 'Work is Dignity'. It's multi-ethnic and bi-sexual and a picture of a lot of depressed looking people going through a door and coming out the other side smiling. Ruth says it's meant to be the social services. Either that or the door leads to a gas chamber and they are all in heaven on the other side.

The community worker designed it. He said he didn't mind me going down to work on it as it was an all women project, but he couldn't pay me as I was not officially on his scheme. I said how could I get on the scheme and he said I couldn't, he had enough girls and the way things were going these days a lad was lucky to get a look in. Ruth says he is a missojinist . . . whatever that is. I looked it up in Nan's crossword dictionary but it doesn't have words as long as that. Probably means something like raasclaat.

Don't worry,
Kim.

Dear Mam,

Shock, horror!

Janice's mum was taken away in an ambulance yesterday. She tried to do herself in again. Janice came home and found her with Errol's football scarf wrapped round her neck and the other end tied to the balcony railings. Janice said it made her so mad she almost pushed her. Janice was crying and saying if she didn't get out of there soon *she'd* be topping herself. She got quite hysterical, but Ruth smacked her face and told her to pull herself together. Ruth can be cruel to be kind sometimes.

I wanted Janice to come and spend the night with me, but she said someone had to be there to iron Errol's tracksuit and her dad would run amok if there wasn't a woman to get his tea. Last time her mother was taken he sawed the legs off the kitchen table. It wouldn't have been so bad but the dinner was on it at the time.

I remember you and dad rowing a lot. But whenever I bring the subject up with Nan, her voice comes over all trembly. She says it was the worst day's work he ever did leaving London and if he hadn't married a Northerner he'd be alive today. She obviously does not know the facts!

Love,
Kim.

Watching Dallas.

WEDNESDAY.

Dear Mam,

I'm sorry I upset you. If you say you and dad had a special relationship I couldn't possibly understand, that is fine by me. Was that before or after dad left home?

The community worker asked me for a date yesterday. His name is Jake and he wears one gold earring. I said I'd go out with him if he could get me on the scheme but he said he couldn't do that, it was more than his job was worth. Ruth got paid her thirty quid today. She gave me a fiver for helping out. She took me to meet her family at teatime. Her mother asked me if I was a Christian. I said I was having an agnostic crisis but I didn't eat meat or believe in nuclear arms. She shook her head and said she'd pray for a conversion.

There's a black cat who keeps coming and sitting on the yard wall. I think he knows there's an 'animal lover' inside. Nan says she won't have a cat in the house, they are smelly and suffocate babies. I wouldn't say I miss home exactly (sorry I missed Mothering Sunday) . . . but it is hard to be a success in London. West Indian people are very friendly but everyone else is too busy to care. I don't know what Mr Tebbit means about getting on your bike. I sold mine to pay for the train fare and I'm worse off than ever!

Love,
Kim.

P.S. I miss you and Dusty of course!

Bed.

SUNDAY.

Dear Mam,

I went out with Jake last night. He took me to a Navant Guard theatre. He said it had a great young people's scheme and I should think about getting involved. I told him I'd had enough of that on the YOPS course. Seemed like a dead end to me. He said that was the trouble with today's youth . . . they were so *nihilistic*.

We saw a play about the end of the world. Jake thought it was great. He said it was 'achingly grave' and he was starving. He took me for a health food pizza and explained that he belonged to a men against sexism group. I said I hoped that didn't mean I had to pay for my own pizza as I was completely skint. But he paid and drove me home right to the door. He said he wouldn't like his sister walking about that late at night.

I fed the black cat tonight. I had to sneak out while Nan was cutting her corns. I gave him a bit of Spam I'd saved from tea. He ate every crumb but ran away when I tried to stroke him.

Goodnight,
Kimmie xx

Dear Tracey,

Thanks for the letter. Sorry I have been a while answering. I am glad you have chucked Naff Nigel, he is a pompous wally. I am going out with a community worker called Jake. His real name is Jason Hope-Lesley but he doesn't tell anyone. He says it's because 'hyphenated names produce class alienation', but I reckon it's because he doesn't want people to laugh.

He has explained all about feminism to me. He reckons it used to be only the 'Loony Left' that called themselves 'Feminists' but now it is OK for everyone, even men. He told me I should raise my consciousness as he was pulling my drainpipes down. He couldn't get them over my ankles (you know how tight those pvc ones are) so as there isn't much room in the front of a Deux Chevaux, he said we'd leave it 'til next time. He's invited me round for 'supper' which is what you have here instead of tea.

All the best,
Kim.

The tin bath in the yard because the sun is shining.

Dear Mam,

Work at last!

Jake told me to go down to the council's training centre and see what they had to offer. I told him I didn't hold out much hope, last time I went there they were carrying out some bloke who'd died in the waiting room. Turned out he'd been there for three days and no-one had noticed. I said, personally, I could think of better ways of doing myself in, than being bored to death by a six page form.

Jake said I was just being cynical and the trouble with today's youth, etc. etc. Anyway, I went down and told a woman I wanted to do car maintenance and she said I could go on a supervised gardening scheme.

She asked me if I'd had any experience and I said I'd once grown a four-leafed clover in a peat pot at school. She said it was more cutting lawns and trimming hedges. I said I hadn't seen any lawns or hedges round us only a dead mucky bush where people dump fried chicken boxes. But she got a bit twitchy so I had to agree I could do window boxes. I am just going down to the garden centre to see what can go in them.

Later.

Do you think a willow tree is a bit big for a box?

> Love,
> Kim.

> The 'potting' shed

Dear Mam,

Yesterday me and Ruth went with Janice to visit her mum. Remember what you were like after dad left? Mrs Webster didn't recognize Janice, even when Janice screamed and bit her arm. Me and Ruth had to hold Janice back and then a nurse came running up and tried to give her an injection. I explained that Janice wasn't a patient, it was just her way of getting her mother's attention, but the nurse took no notice and went on jabbing Janice's leg, so in the end Ruth had to hit her and her nose bled all over her NHS pinny. I tried to calm everyone down but by this time the nurse was screaming as well and Ruth was shouting ~~raaselaat~~ that word I told you about last time. Janice cried all the way home. She wouldn't even cheer up when Ruth brought out the chocolate she'd taken for Mrs Webster. I thought Ruth was a bit mean not to have left it at the hospital but she said what was the point . . . Mrs Webster was too far gone to know the difference between a Rollo and a Rolex. She reckons it's the pills they give you in there.

As I was walking up our street I saw Mr Bibby, who lives over the road, struggling with his shopping. I ran up to help him but he hit me with his walking stick. When he saw that it was me he apologized. He said he thought I was going to mug him. You couldn't be too careful these days – Mrs Salmon had had her Barnardo's box stolen by a youth on Community Service who came to clean the windows. When I told Nan about it she said it would serve him right if he was mugged, he was a mean old bugger and always cheated at whist.

The black cat was sitting by the back door when I went to put some bread out for the birds. He looked at me and I looked at him. He's very dirty and only has half an ear on one side. Nan wasn't in the kitchen so I gave him some Long Life out of the jug. He drank it up very fast then he lifted his tail and peed all over the coal shed door. I think he likes me.

Love,
Kim.

TUESDAY.

Dear Mam,

I'm sorry my last letter upset you. Of course I do not go round telling people you are a loony. I just mentioned it to Janice to cheer her up. Mrs Webster is much worse than you . . . the only time I thought you were not yourself was when I found you with your head in the gas oven. I know you were only giving the back a good clean but it was a bit worrying to come in and find all the doors and windows shut and a note saying don't light any matches. By the way, I think you should be careful what you say about dad in the rest of your letters. Nan found the last one down the side of the armchair and she read it before I could snatch it away. When she got to the bit about 'lying adulterous bastard', she turned a funny·colour and started to choke. I managed to get a bottle of Milk Stout down her throat and explained that you couldn't really be blamed for thinking dad was a bit of a pillock when he'd left you for the barmaid at 'The Fighting Cock'. At first she wouldn't believe me, then she muttered something about not getting it from her side of the family.

I went round to see Janice today. Errol was in bed with his leg in a plaster cast. He had an accident on his motor bike. Well, not exactly *on* it, he doesn't ride it as you know, but he was tinkering with it outside the Tower when a police car with its siren going came swerving round the corner. It lifted Errol clean into the air and carried him on the bonnet up the road and twice round the roundabout. That would have been alright because Errol managed to hang on to the windscreen wipers. But when the driver noticed him, he did an emergency stop and Errol lost his grip and shot into the one-way sign. He broke his leg in fifteen places and the police officer. charged him with obstruction. He is supposed to go to court on Wednesday, but he'll have to go by ambulance – the hospital didn't have any crutches on account of 'the cuts'. Janice was playing Snap with him so I went out to do the shopping, it took me ages as the lift's still out of order. Janice keeps phoning the Council but the Housing Officer's in a meeting. She says it must be a ~~bloody~~ very long meeting she has phoned him twenty-eight times since Friday.

I got us beans on toast and after we ate it everyone

cheered up. Janice said she might come out on Saturday.
There is a parade in the park.

Love,
Kim.

P.S. Don't say pillock if you're talking to the vicar.

Dear Tracey,

'Supper' consisted of seaweed soup with yoghurt and soya
bean rissoles. What came after was rubbish as well. An
hour and a half lecture on the martial arts and then a
wrestle on his Afghan rug. I tried to get into it 'cos Jake
said it was 'provincial' to be scared of passion, but he had
a bit of whole wheat stuck between his teeth and every time
I looked at him I burst out laughing. Jake said I was
obviously not in touch with my body and recommended a
session with Alexander, whoever he is. Probably another
nut crunching maniac. Jake told me to think it over and
ring him when I'd decided to 'reach a mature understanding'. Bloody Nora!

Kim.

The dentist's waiting room.

MONDAY.

Dear Mam,

I gave Nan the notelet you sent her with the picture of
Lancaster Castle. Fortunately, it doesn't mention that it's
used as a prison now. She didn't say much but I think she
was pleased. She is using it as a bookmark in 'Plantaganet

Idylls' which I got her from the library. She doesn't think it's much of a story, she prefers Romantic Fiction, but they only had 'The Boston Strangler' and I wasn't sure that counted.

Yes, we did go to the park. We took Nan with us but there were so many policemen it was hard for her to see. Ruth and I took it in turns to have her on our shoulders, but she worried about people being able to see her knickers and she said police on horses made her 'agitato'. It reminded her of when they chased starving people in the General Strike. Janice said they still do that round her council estate, only now they have got patrol cars. It snowed a bit and as Janice is dead nesh we went home and celebrated the end of Lent with four brown ales and a Kit-kat.

I got a letter from the training centre today. I'm going on my first gardening job in the morning. The funny thing is it's only over the road. It's Mr Bibby's address which I can't understand as I've never seen anything green round his house. Nan was furious. She said if Mr Bibby could call that pile of junk a garden then she was going to put soil in the zinc bath and get the council round with some horse manure. Actually, she didn't say 'manure'. I had to promise to make her a rockery before she would calm down. Flippin' 'eck!

I have christened the black cat Marvin after Marvin Gaye. They have both had violent lives.

Kim.

P.S. The rag and bone man's just been round. I have given him the zinc bath and a carrot.

Dear Mam,

It was a root filling. An All Bran biscuit broke my wisdom tooth in half.

Thanks for the picture of Dusty. Funny ... she looks dead small. Marvin comes round for his tea every day now. I gave him some sardines Nan had left in the fridge yesterday and she went mad. She said she was saving them for snap at the Whist Drive. Her and Mrs Salmon always take their own because the community centre caff only has onion bhajees. I pointed out to her that she is living in a multi-ethnic society and how would an Indian lady like a cheese and pickle sandwich?

The gardening assignment was OK. The 'prune dead wood' was chopping up a shed and the 'clear waste' was unblocking the drains. After I'd finished Mr Bibby invited me in for a cup of tea. He showed me his collection of World War One medals and while I was bending over them he put his hand on my bottom. He must be ninety if he's a day! Nan says he is a dirty old git and well known for it at the Whist drive. She and Mrs Salmon always wear two pairs of knickers in case they get him on their table.

Mrs Salmon has arranged for me to go and meet her son Reg. He is the one who runs the garage. He wants a part-time assistant. From no jobs to two in under a week, things are looking up! It's Nan's birthday next week and she's been dropping hints about her present. She wants a two-speed microwave with self-set facilities. She's getting a pair of slippers.

Love,
Kim.

P.S. I don't know if he's vegetarian. The carrot was for his horse.

Bed.

Dear Mam,

Went to meet Reg Salmon. It was a bit of a shock. It's not a garage he runs it is a scrap yard. There are no petrol pumps, only rows and rows of rubber tyres and a mountain of bashed Cortinas. I'd dressed up specially in my chain mail T-shirt and studded leather coat. He fell about laughing when he saw me, yet he was wearing an ancient oily boilersuit and filthy-looking shirt! What a way for a manager to dress! He is supposed to set an example!

When he'd finished wiping his eyes on a bit of tarry rag he said, 'I'm Reg Salmon, my friends call me Scotch. Come on in and I'll show you what to do.' He took me into a smelly little hut, overflowing with bits of paper, and said, 'If you can make any sense of that lot, it's twenty-five quid and as much free scrap as you can carry away.' Just my flippin' luck, a desk job! I was there from 9 o'clock 'til half past five and I still hadn't found the desk! I could *die* in that hut suffocated by paper and I wouldn't be found for a hundred years. Scotch only came in for cups of tea and to crack unfunny jokes about my appearance. He asked me if I smoked when he was rolling a cig and when I said I did he offered me a butt end from behind his ear. Some people are so mean!

He gave me a tenner at the end of the day and a lift home in his mucky E-Type. I had to put a newspaper over the seat, it looked as though someone had been sick on it.

I am going in again on Friday.

Your exhausted daughter,
Kim.

Dear Tracey,

I am now being felt up by my boss, who is old enough to be my dad! Fortunately, I can move faster than he can, being twelve stone lighter. Me zip-ups seem to have an irresistible fascination for men down here, they can't wait to get their hands inside. Scotch managed one finger the other day but I pulled up the zip and nearly cut it off. He didn't half scream.

I've bought the new 'Eurythmics' album with my first week's pay. Seen! (West Indian for F.A.B.)

Kim.

Bed. Friday

Dear Mum,

sorry it's only a postcard. I was so tired when I got in after a day wrestling with Scotch Salmon's VAT, I couldn't face a letter. I have cut two felt pens, a biro and my eyebrow pencil on the books today. And I have to provide my own. A working pen is completely alien to that so-called 'office'. Scotch uses them all to stir his tea. Thanks for the M+S undies, I will save them for days that I get knocked down crossing the road.

Princess Diana being presented with a giant squid for 'Will's aquarium.

Ho Ho!

yawn, Kim ✗

Mrs. Kirby

Lakeland

Wordsworth Walk

off London road

34

Nan's armchair.

MONDAY.

Dear Mam,

A *proper* letter.

Saturday I went to Mr Bibby's in the morning. He wanted me to give a lick of paint to his garden gnome. I was a bit surprised as he hasn't got a garden, but he explained it was to go on the display unit where he keeps his Home Guard uniform – khaki long johns, a battered tin hat and a shrunken head from his desert campaign. He wanted something in keeping with the military flavour so I gave it one eye, one arm and a row of medals. He wasn't very grateful. I don't know why he didn't do it himself. The room is full of pictures he says he painted. They are mostly women with camels or donkeys. I suppose they are from his desert campaign too. I had to stand on a chair to put the gnome in place and just as I was stretching up he grabbed me round the knees. It was such a surprise I dropped the gnome on his head. Fortunately it didn't knock him out, but he reeled around a bit so I put the pair of long johns soaked in water on his head.

In the afternoon I went by tube to Oxford Circus. We were stuck in a tunnel for forty-five minutes. Nobody spoke but a few people had to wipe beads of sweat off their foreheads. We never found out what was wrong but according to Jake it is all to do with the infrastructure. I don't know what that is but apparently it's crumbling. I hope I am not down a tube when it finally caves in. A fight broke out on the 'up' escalator. Luckily, my fall was broken by four large football fans who were all crammed on a step, singing 'We'll Never Walk Alone'. No sooner had I retrieved Nan's plastic string bag from the 'down' escalator, than I was accosted by beggars. The first was a hippy saying 'Peace and Love' to the people rushing by. He got a bit aggressive when I told him I didn't have any change.

35

The second was a 'war veteran' selling Union Jack matches. He got people's attention by cracking them across the back of their legs with his walking stick and killing himself laughing. I don't think that is the way to sell many matches but I must say he had a good sense of humour for a man with no legs.

I bought Nan a lovely pair of slippers with pompoms on the front and a set of Uri Geller spoons from the British Rail Lost Property shop. I just had enough left to get a flea collar for Marvin. Nan says she's not stopped scratching since he came into the house.

Must finish as I've got to plant the rockery before meeting Ruth and Janice for a ~~drink~~ walk in the park.

Love,
Kim.

The shed,
'Salmon's Scrap',
Knackers Yard (Unadopted)

FRIDAY

Dear Mam,

What *is* the matter? I can't seem to tell you *anything* these days without you going off the deep end! The fight on the escalator was nothing to do with me. It was started by two skinheads. I just happened to be standing between them at the time. I had a lucky escape, the man next to me had his handbag ripped to shreds, I only lost a nose stud and the lining of my jacket.

As for drink ... I have only been inside 'The Jolly Cockney' once, and that was to pick up Nan the night she had four Snowballs. I suppose I *will* have to report Mr Bibby to the council if he tries it on again, but I don't think he *meant* to put his hand up my skirt. He said the chair was wobbling and he thought I might fall. He's asked me to sit for him to show he's really sorry.

Nan liked her slippers but she wasn't very impressed with the Uri Geller spoons. She said there was nothing special about them, all British Rail cutlery was like that. I have given them to Scotch for scrap. Your card arrived today. Only two days late. Nan has put it on the mantel piece next to the pile of final demands. Must stop, can hear Scotch's hobnailed boots crunching over the spare parts to the shed.

Kim.

Later.

Have just got home and found all the rockery plants dead! Nan says it is because Marvin peed in them but Jake says it was probably caused by 'acid rain'. So don't go out in the wet unless you put a bag over your head!

FRIDAY.

Dear Tracey,

Can you go round and have a look at me mam? I think she's going funny in the head again. She keeps bleatin' on about rape and murder in London, though I've told her the nearest molesting was at least three streets away. (Not counting Mr Bibby who has asked to paint me topless.) I'd come home for a weekend but I haven't got the fare.

All the best,
Kim.

P.S. Yes I'm still going out with Jake. But we haven't reached a 'mature understanding' yet. I'm still clamping me thighs together when he tries to get his fingers through the holes in me fishnet tights.

S. S. Doberman,
Head of Kennels,
Metropolitan Police Authority,
Hendon.

FRIDAY.

Dear Sir,

In reference to your advert in 'The Sunday Express', I would like to apply for the post of 'Experienced Dog Handler'.

I have not had my own dog since I was six and our mongrel was shot for stealing next door's budgie (she only wanted to play), but I have had recent experience with a Jack Russell terrier. My friend Janice's next door neighbour's baby was left in a flat with it. Fortunately, we heard the noise and when we broke down the door we found the baby being dragged across the floor by her teething ring. Neither she nor the dog would let go. Janice got Conan by the tail and I forced a boot between his jaws. When the neighbour came back she was furious about the door. She said it was only Conan's way of having fun and anyway the baby was twice his size. I sustained a tooth hole in my Doc Martin and also my foot which was in it at the time. But this does not deter me. I have watched all Barbara Woodhouse's programmes on TV and am now teaching Conan to sit-ta!

Yours very faithfully,
Kim Kirby.

Bed.

WEDNESDAY.

Dear Mam,

I have met a rich person at last! Her name is Mrs Gumbolling and she's married to Mr Gumbolling who is a writer. The rest of the time he works for a newspaper. They live in a four storey house in Clapham and I know they are rich because I saw an avocado on top of the fridge. Also, Mrs Gumbolling, who has a funny foreign accent, said she would give me a bit extra if I'd clean all the dog poo off the garden path, although it wasn't in the job description, which was: 'Cut lawn, trim hedge, feed goldfish'. It's the biggest patch of grass I've seen in London, you can lie full length on it – I know because Mrs Gumbolling was while I was trying to cut it. When it came to 'trim hedge', I couldn't find any equipment. Mrs Gumbolling looked vague but said she would find me something. After a while she came back with a pair of nail scissors. She's obviously barking. She was wearing leg warmers even though it was really hot today.

Later she brought me some ants' eggs and said it was dead easy, all I had to do was sprinkle them on the pond. She'd do it herself but she was allergic to fish. I was still there when Mr Gumbolling came in from work (3.30). He looked very hot and bothered and didn't even say hello when he bumped into me humping a sack of dog do to the dustbin. Mrs Gumbolling said not to worry he was very shy and had a horror of human contact. She dealt with everything practical. She gave me 50p.

I have now got three jobs but am as poor as ever! I wasn't reckoning on Nan's birthday tea costing quite so much. She invited everyone from her lunch club. Thirty-four OAPs and three dogs can get through a lot of sausages on sticks. I've got a crippling backache (never try to cut a

39

hedge with a Swiss Army knife) and I've got to go to Scotch's first thing in the morning.

Nan sends regards,
Kim.

The bath

Dear Mam,

Scotch Salmon's son Cheyenne was at the yard today. He's just come out of a short sharp shock centre and Scotch said he didn't recognize him when he first came home. He now has very short hair and no front teeth. He says they offered him a short back and sides and removed his teeth when he said no thank you. Scotch says he's going to write to his MP.

I got Ruth to come and help me with the shed. She said the best thing to do was to make a bonfire of it all and start again from scratch. Cheyenne came up and said his dad had told him to help but when he saw the amount there was to carry, he said why didn't we take a short cut and set fire to the shed? He grabbed a can of petrol and was just about to chuck it when Scotch screeched up in the red E-Type. I won't go into details but I will say I never thought a twenty-stone alcoholic would be able to move so fast. After Cheyenne had climbed out of the car crusher he said he'd never had a shock as bad as that inside! I have been given a 'strong warning', which consisted of Scotch picking me up by my shoulder pads and shaking me 'til all my chains rattled. It seems a bit unfair. How was I to know Cheyenne was sent to the detention centre for setting fire to the DHSS? I've had a week's pay docked. I'll never be able to open an account at the listening bank at this rate!

Your fed-up daughter,
Kim.

Mr G. Nash,
Ground Floor,
Oral House,
Lambeth

Dear Mr Nash,

I would like to apply for 'Trainee Dental Nurse with Full Chairside Duties'. Looking in people's mouths is fascinating. My cat yawned the other day and I could see right down to the liver he'd had for dinner.

I am very used to chairside duties as I live with an OAP. Once she has sat down for the evening she doesn't budge 'til bedtime. It's 'run and fetch me this' and 'just bring me that'. If I complain she says I've got young legs. Which they won't be for much longer!

I can come for an interview any time.

Yours willingly,
Kim Kirby.

TUESDAY.

Dear Mam,

You are right. It's not like me to give up. Though the odds are a bit against me becoming an international financier (Nan's ambition for me) or even a car mechanic at the moment.

Things are looking up, though. I have applied to go on a course of Motor Mechanics. It's all women and run by the council. I had to fill in a form and though I don't have *all* the qualifications, I think I will do alright. It's either that or emigrating to New Zealand. They are Nuclear Free but Ruth says she'd rather be incinerated than live in a country where there are more sheep than people. Jake says he prefers sheep to people.

Kim.

41

APPLICATION FORM

Women's Motor Mechanics Scheme
The Basement
Wombwell Grove

Applicant for Course of Women's Motor Mechanics

Are you
1) An ex-prisoner?......*NO*................................
2) Black?......*NO*................................
3) Any other Ethnic Minority? ....*NO*..............
4) Single parent lesbian? .....*NO*................
5) Disabled lesbian?.....*N.O*................
6) Lesbian?....*DON'T KNOW*................
7) Working class?.....*NEARLY*................
8) Do you have your own tool?....*E.H.?*..........

Signature

Kim Kirby ♀

The front step

SUNDAY.

Dear Mam,

Don't be daft. Of course I am not going to New Zealand. The fare is £1,317.

It's really nice today. Nan and I have had a walk by the duck pond. She got very 'agitato' this morning as she couldn't find her knickers. She hung them out on the line yesterday and this morning they were gone. She says that is the second pair this week. No-one in their right mind would steal Nan's knickers, they are size XL pale green interlock and come down to her knees. She says people who steal knickers are not in their right mind.

42

Went to the Gumbollings' again on Friday. She asked me if I'd clean her windows. When I walked up the front door was open and the Gumbollings were in the hall having a row. Mr Gumbolling shouted, 'Irina, you are full of rancorous man-hatred,' and Mrs Gumbolling screamed, 'Gordon you are full of shit!' Then Mr Gumbolling stormed out of the house, shoving me into the ornamental rosebed. Mrs Gumbolling said he was always like this on a Friday because of his weekend deadline. I looked up rancorous but Nan's dictionary only had rancid, which means smelling of stale fat. Perhaps he was referring to her face cream. She gave me £2 and a tin of smoked oysters. I didn't fancy them and Nan said she'd rather have a whelk so we gave them to Marvin for his tea.

I am glad you have joined the Amateur Operatics, you ought to get out and about more. After all, you are not bad looking and not that old. Gigi *was* supposed to be 15 though wasn't she?

Kim x

FRIDAY.

Dear Mam,

I did not say shit. Mrs Gumbolling said it. I've heard Mr Gumbolling say much worse than that but I don't know how to spell the words he uses. The other day he threw his typewriter out of the window. Mrs Gumbolling was in a bikini and legwarmers doing yoga on the lawn. It landed right by her head just as she was standing on it. She didn't even wobble. Later on she explained that Mr Gumbolling was having a writer's crisis.

At lunchtime she asked me if I wanted a drink. I said yes and she brought me a large vodka. I said what I really meant was a cup of tea, so she gave me something horrible in a Chinese cup. She said it was made by Earl Grey. I don't know when he made it but it tasted as if it had been

standing in the pot for a week. Mr Gumbolling came down for lunch. He didn't say anything except 'aren't there any anchovies?' Mrs Gumbolling says he has got very eesoterick tastes. I think that must mean foreign, as he married her.

Of course I remember Gary Prescott. He used to run a spitting competition on the school bus. Mr Bakewell said he was the most foul-mouthed boy in the school. He and Gordon Gumbolling could have a competition! Fancy him playing bass in the band. He has fancied himself as a performer ever since Miss De'Ath had him as a torso in Titus Andronicus. He used to rub himself in a bucket of pigs' kidneys every night before he came on stage.

Must go now. I have promised to take Conan and Janice for a walk.

Love,
Kim.

P.S. I didn't know Gigi was a rock opera?

Dear Tracey,

Thanks a lot for calling on me mam. I'm glad she seemed so cheery. It *is* unusual for her to be drinking Babycham at 4.30 in the afternoon. Did Gary Prescott stay after you left?

Don't breathe a word but I have been down to the family planning clinic. I am getting fed up of Jake ruining all me tights. Me fishnets have got holes a giant cod could swim through. Ruth took me down. She said I might as well get the first one over and then I could start to enjoy it. I have got a leaflet that tells you what to do. The most important thing is 'Never boil your diaphragm'.

K.!

The swimming baths

SATURDAY.

Dear Mam,

Of course I realize rehearsals take up a lot of time. I didn't ring because I was worried, I just thought it would be nice to have a chat. Gary Prescott sounds just the same. No, Tracey did not mention you were rehearsing 'The Night They Invented Champagne' when she came round. I suppose the four Babychams were to put you in the mood. By the way, when did you dye your hair ash blonde?

I've had a very busy week. I had three sittings for Mr Bibby. For the first one I was fully dressed. Did I mention it is dead hot here? Ruth and Janice and me have been to the swimming baths a lot. Janice won't come in the water as she says it can give you Aids, so she sits on the side and chats to the life guard. Ruth is a great swimmer. The other day I was lying on my back practising the butterfly stroke when Damien (the life guard) started the wave machine.

45

My waterwings were ripped off me in seconds and I would have drowned if it hadn't been for Ruth. Fortunately she'd been practising picking bricks up from the bottom. Ruth called Damien a ~~raaeeaat~~ an annoying person but he just grinned. He was showing off for Janice.

I've also been working a lot. Mrs Gumbolling asked me to spray her greenfly and gave me some yellow stuff in a bottle. It was very effective, all the leaves on the rose tree curled up and turned brown. Mrs Gumbolling told me afterwards it was the only thing she'd ever known work, it had such a high percentage of alcohol. Later I found a bell jar of it in the shed. It was labelled 'Gordon's urine'.

Please write and tell me all about Gigi. Mrs Rowbottom certainly does seem to have some very original ideas. For a vicar's wife.

Kim.

WEDNESDAY.

Dear Mam,

Thanks for the card. It's not Christmas for another six months though. Thanks for the postal order as well, I'm saving up to get Nan some new thermal combinations. Her last lot were nicked off the line. Whoever is doing it must be going to climb Everest as the temperature here is 83 degrees.

When does Gigi start? I hope you will not be bitterly disappointed with your criticisms. The other day I found Irina Gumbolling in tears in the study. She was surrounded by yellowing bits of newspaper. She kept picking pieces up and reading them and then clutching them to her chest (what there is of it) and crying loudly. I was a bit embarrassed as I'd only gone up to find out if she wanted the begonias potting on. But she made me sit down and listen while she read bits out. She kept saying 'Oh what a

46

bastard'. Later I found out she was talking about a critic who had written on her dancing in a ballet called 'Gazelle'. He said she was 'like Olive Oyl, a beansprout with thick ankles'. She said she'd accept Olive Oyl and beansprout but thick ankles was going too far. No wonder she always wears leg warmers. I did'nt realize she was a ballet dancer but that explains her foreign accent and also why she can put her legs behind her head.

I hope your critic is not such a nasty person. We don't want you committing suicide after the first night!

Kim.

Tea table.

TUESDAY.

Dear Mam,

Of course I didn't mean that you have got thick ankles. Anyway they won't show as you'll be wearing a long frock. I am sure you will be great in it and Kent Pedlar will not dare say anything against you in the Evening Argos. He better not or I'll tell everyone I saw him chatting up a 13 year old behind our school bike shed. I quite understand that you'd need extra rehearsals as it's a long time since you've sung. I can't remember you opening your mouth since dad left, which is funny as he always used to tell you to put a sock in it when you started on 'Yesterday'. It's very nice of Gary Prescott to come round and give you a hand. Does he still pick his nose?

It is dead hot here. It's sweltering in Scotch Salmon's shed. The other day I just had to strip off even though I was only wearing a string vest and footless tights to start with, and just as I was removing my nose stud Scotch's wife Tara came in. She gave me a funny look, but after all it is not my fault if she's married to a sex-crazed pervert

47

who chases people round the yard with a crank shaft in his hand. One of these days he will have a heart attack.

She said where was Scotch, this new car was giving her grief, the engine had seized up. I said Scotch was with a client (I did not mention it was the barman at 'The Jolly Cockney') but *I* would have a look. She screeched with laughter and said Scotch would have a fit, *she* wasn't allowed to lift the bonnet. I said in that case it wasn't surprising there was no oil in the engine. She gave me a funny look and after I'd filled it she drove off in a cloud of exhaust fumes, knocking down a police cone and an OAP.

Must finish as I'm taking Nan to the Junction to buy some new roll-ons.

Love,
Kim.

The shed
Knacker's Yard

MONDAY.

Dear Mam,

No the OAP wasn't hurt, just a bit stunned. I gave her a cup of tea out of Scotch's flask and she said she felt much better. I am not surprised. I had a cup to keep her company and now I know where Scotch got his nickname.

Nan is made up. We got her two pairs of thermal knickers, a vest, a petticoat and some pink rubber roll-ons. She hasn't had them off since. She says the only way to make sure they're not nicked is to wear them all the time. She's convinced it is Mr Bibby and wants me to search his drawers next time I go to weed his front doorstep. Your money came in dead handy and Nan was really touched. Of course I didn't tell her you said, 'get yourself a decent meal, the old bag always was a terrible cook.'

I am glad your rehearsals are going so well. I'm sure it's Miss De'Ath and not you that cannot find top C. She was always playing bum notes in assembly. Her favourite hymn was 'Will Your Anchor Hold'. She used to eyeball Mr Bakewell when she played it. Funny that so many people from my old school are in 'Gigi'. Why have they hung around? Mr Bakewell always used to urge people to travel in his end of year speech. But I suppose he had his reasons. He used to say travel broadens the mind. It's true, I'd never have had a black best friend if I had stayed up there, though I must say it is rather rude of Miss De'Ath to ask if I have become a drug addict or had a baby yet.

Must stop as I think Cheyenne is coming. The ginger cat has just shot past the window with a lager can tied to its tail.

Bye!
Kim.

Christabel De'Ath
'Nightingale' Cottage
Hyperian Hill
Off London Rd.   TUESDAY

Dear Miss De'Ath,

It is very kind of you to enquire about me. No, I have not done any theatricals since I have been down here, I have been too busy looking for a proper job. Every day I get up and look out at the grimy streets of London. They are pewter grey, sometimes flecked with chocolate brown where dogs have passed by. I yawn, stretch and have my breakfast. Some golden corn flakes with ~~ice~~ creamy milk and sugar. When I have finished Marvin my coal black cat licks

49

the bowl clean. I kiss my Nan goodbye and go to work. Sometimes it is to a ~~scorched~~ luscious Clapham garden, where I prune the Magenta Hibiscus, sometimes to a ~~dirty~~ dear old man across the road where I throw pungent pine disinfectant down the lav...atory and sometimes to a 'vehicle relocation centre' where I am in charge of a ~~shed~~ office and spend the day doing ~~the crossword~~ important paper work and chatting to the proprietor and his ~~friends~~ clients.

In the evening I return home and have a relaxing soak in the kitchen. Nan reads the paper and we discuss world affairs. Who Joan Collins is divorcing now and whether Fergie is pregnant or not. Sometimes I accompany her to Bingo or Whist where I meet friends and go for a ~~drink~~ walk. Later we return and watch television until Nan falls asleep. Then it is a soothing cup of tea and bed with a good book. 'I married a Werewolf' or 'Lesbian Nation'.

On Saturdays I shop and bargain merrily with the street traders and Sunday is a high spot when we pop down to St Agnes the Martyr.

Yours faithfully,
Kim Kirby

SUNDAY

Dear Mam,

I am sorry Miss De'Ath couldn't come to rehearsals for three days after my letter but I can't understand what put her in such a state. I tried to remember all the rules of composition she taught us, use colourful adjectives, put in the odd surprise, I even used some words from the dictionary so I know the spelling was OK. If you ask me she is barking. I remember she made me stand in the corner once because I wrote 'Mummy and Daddy did not speak for a week after Mummy called Daddy a rotten shit' in 'What I did on my holidays' and she always used to cry

50

when she was reading 'Ode to a Nightingale'. 'He was so young so young' she used to murmur. Talking of which, have you had any more private rehearsals with Gary Prescott?

Love,
Kim.

P.S. I *didn't* do it on purpose to upset the show.

THURSDAY.

Dear Mother,

What do you mean, nasty and unkind remarks? I don't mind you having a good time at all. If you want to go around with dyed hair drinking Malibu and pineapple with a ~~creep~~ lad who gave Marilyn Braithwaite impetigo it's nothing to do with me. You're old enough (39½) to make up your own mind.

I cannot write any longer as I've got to take Marvin to the vet. He is going bald. Nan says it is his age.

Kim.

Dear Mother,

Tracey told me actually. She saw you in 'Gropers' wine bar with Gary, but she was probably exaggerating when she said he had his hand half way down the front of your T-shirt. I have bought you an early Christmas present at St Agnes Arts and Crafts fair. It is a nice flannel nightie.

Best wishes,
Kim.

The 'potting' shed.

SUNDAY.

Dear Tracey,

Thanks for keeping an eye on me mam. I think she is going prematurely senile. Though come to think of it she *is* nearly forty.

Thanks for the photo. The Princess Di haircut is dead fashionable *here*. Even Nan's home help has got one.

I have been down to the family planning clinic again to get fitted for a diagram. Dr Cadoza made me lie on a couch with my legs up in the air. It was dead embarrassing especially as we hardly knew each other. She kept chatting on about the heatwave and shoving freezing cold things up me. If the real thing is anything like that I shall be using me cap to grow mustard and cress with. I shan't need it this weekend as Jake is going to a conference on sexuality awareness.

!

Kim.

Dear Mother,

I am sorry to hear a bee got trapped in your bra. It was kind of Gary to get it out. I do hope he wasn't stung.

Mrs Webster came home from hospital today. It's shutting down its phsychiatric wing. Janice and me and Ruth went to get her. It's obvious Mrs Webster is not better. She was wearing moon boots, three jumpers, ear muffs and a scarf though the temperature today was the highest ever recorded. Mrs Webster is 39½ (like you) but she looks about 50 (what you can see of her). Ruth said it was the result of building her life around men. She was bound to be disappointed. Janice said she didn't agree, it was her place to be a wife and mother. She said Damien was so big and strong he made her feel tiny and helpless. Ruth said she'd give her a cage for her bottom drawer as she wanted to be a gerbil.

Good luck for Thursday. What a shame it's only on for three performances. Irina Gumbolling says dancers tell each other to break a leg, but in Gary's case I suppose it should be a string.

Kim.

McDonald's

SATURDAY.

Dear Mam,

I'm glad you have had such a success. Trust Kent Pedlar to say you looked every inch the fifteen year old. He should know, he has been over every inch behind the Junior school bike shed.

I suppose things are back to normal now?

I have been asked to catsit for Mr and Mrs Gumbolling.

They're going on a weekend break for Mrs Gumbolling's nerves. She has been in a very bad way since she was arrested for shoplifting.

Their cats are Siamese twins called Titipoo and Yum Yum and I'm not very keen on them as Yum Yum peed all over my gardening wellies. Irina said she was only being friendly and they were the most delightful animals when you got to know them. But I saw Mr Gumbolling pick Titipoo up by his neck the other day and shake him out of the window. It's lucky he wasn't having another writer's crisis as the garden was two floors down.

I said I would do it if Ruth could stay as well but I didn't fancy spending the weekend with Dooarneeay Roussoh. Irina said she would think about it.

Love,
Kim.

WEDNESDAY.

Dear Tracey,

No we haven't done it yet. Jake is having a 'celibacy crisis'. It was that conference. He said his eyes had been opened to 'alternative sensual options'. We're going to a lot of art exhibitions instead. You say you saw me mam at a *rock* concert? She must have been with the St Johns or something. Was she wearing a uniform?

Love,
Kim.

P.S. Do not go on the pill whatever Nigel says. Ruth says you'll have cancer by the time you are forty. Still, I suppose it won't matter by then.

Dear Mam,

Irina Gumbolling is not a 'hardened criminal'. She just has funny turns when she's been reading her rotten reviews. She says her mind goes a blank and when she comes to there she is outside Sainsbury's clutching a packet of Chinese chicken wings. I suppose they are for Gordon's eesoterick taste. Mr Gumbolling was furious with her. He said if this gets into the papers he will be finished. I don't see why. He reads things like 'Man exposes himself in ice cream parlour' out of the Guardian every day and sniggers to himself.

I took Ruth round to meet Irina. When we got there she was feeding the Sunday papers to the vegetable shredder. Gordon has forbidden her to read them any more. He says they're designed to provoke rage and bilious envy. I think he must be right as Irina suddenly bent over making horrible retching noises. She had just caught sight of a picture of Ludmilla Tretchikova, her archest thin-ankled rival. They were students in Moscow together but Ludmilla was blonde and the girl friend of a general. The review said she danced 'Like divine spun sugar, every gesture a triumph of blithely subtle allure.' Irina said she was about as subtle as a

Она также грациозна как корова на льду.

which is Russian for a blow on the head with a flat iron. It was a good thing Ruth was with me, as Irina turned purple and started to foam at the mouth. Ruth got her in a half-Nelson and forced her head between her knees. She was the first Girl Guide in her company to get her advanced badge in First Aid.

The Gumbollings are going away on Friday. Ruth is allowed to stay. They are giving me ten pounds and taking Doo-arnier Russo with them.

Love,
Kim.

P.S. Doo-arnier Russo is their dog.

Gordon's Parker Knoll Leather Chair

SATURDAY.

Dear Tracey,

What did you mean, not unless you call a gold lamé halterneck and satin disco pants a uniform? My mother wouldn't be seen dressed like that. She buys all her clothes from Marks & Spencers. It must have been someone else. No we still haven't done it. I am getting worried, at this rate the rubber will be perished.

Kim.

TUESDAY.

Dear Mam,

Yes, Tracey said she'd seen you doing the twist in satin disco trousers. Was cyclamen the only colour they had? I am sure they look fab. Of course they do show every bump.

Yes thanks, I enjoyed my stay at the Gumbollings', though Nan said it made her 'agitato' to be by herself (I don't know why, she was by herself for 83 years before I came). It rained rather a lot, which was a shame as the Gumbollings had gone to the Norfolk Broads. Mrs Gumbolling left Ruth and me a list of instructions as thick as a telephone directory.

1) Water Basil (I do not know who Basil is but we didn't find him all weekend).

2) Collect 'Observer' from hall floor before cats have time to tinkle on it.

3) Be super sure about security. Gordon has had his word processor stolen five times. Last time the vandals left something unspeakable in its place.

4) Do not allow Yum Yum to eat the birds she catches. They give her colic. If she *is* sick you will usually find it on Gordon's pillow.

We had a great time though. We played all their compact discs. Ruth wore Gordon's ear plugs as they were mostly opera. We watched their video tapes (all of the Bolshoi ballet, Irina must have to be tied to a chair when Gordon puts those on!). Took it in turns to have a jacuzzi bath and slept in their waterbed.

By the way I have found out what eesoterick means.

Love,
Kim.

Dear Mother,

That is *not* what eesoterick means. Ruth and I *didn't* sleep together as Irina and Gordon have *separate* waterbeds. I slept in Gordon's. I knew it was his because there was a typewriter on the bedside table and a pile of notes. They must have been for his novel as the first line began 'He lay on the bed in a miasma of melancholy . . .' On his shelf was a photograph album. I thought it might have some pictures of Irina dancing 'Gazelle' and I wanted to see if she really did have thick ankles, so I had a look. I will not say any more except I was very surprised by what I saw. I never knew you could buy underwear like that. Let alone for men. Also, I do not see why Irina says Gordon has a horror of human contact!

How nice of Gary to invite you to his 'gig'. Do they still call them that up there?

Must go. Nan is shouting me. She has got stuck to the lavatory seat again.

Yours,
Kim.

Irina's Utility Room

FRIDAY.

Dear Tracey,

I am working for *another* pervert! He dresses up in women's underwear! I have seen a load of pictures of him and his wife and all I can say is it's a good job she's double jointed! I will never be able to look them in the eye again. Not now I've looked them in every other part. It's enough to put you off sex for life. Fortunately Jake is still drinking herb tea and meditating.

On Sunday he took me to see some statues by a man called Rodin. It was very crowded. The biggest statue had a load of blokes round it all drawing furiously. I felt like calling 'come in your time is up'. Jake said its title was 'The Thinker' and it had 'tremendous strength'. I said it would need it to stay in that position long. He said the man was 'lost in a swirling metaphor of pain'. I said it must have been constipation as he looked like he needed a crap.

There were lots of drawings of women. 'Iris, Messenger of the Gods' was showing everything she'd got and there were several girls with their legs behind their heads, just like the photos in Gordon Gumbolling's album. It is obviously a fashion. When we got to the 'The Kiss' Jake stared at it for ages. He said it had a 'gloriously voluptuous line'. But when I said the bloke reminded me of Rambo, Jake got cross and said I had no visual sense. After he had looked at it from every angle including upside down (Jake not the statue) he clutched himself and said he had a desperate gnawing hunger. We went to the cafe and he ate three bowls of muesli. I don't think these alternative options are working out for Jake.

Later we went to another art place to see some 'collarges' of pavements. There was one entitled 'Northern Kerb-stone'. It was broken and mucky with a load of litter round it. It made me feel dead homesick. I liked it much better than the statues which I thought were rude. But I didn't say so in case Jake said I was 'provincial' again.

Puzzled,
Kim.

Dear Mother,

As far as I know neither Mr nor Mrs Gumbolling has a prison record. Anyway you can talk. Gary Prescott got 21 hours community service for nicking bondage mags from the travelling library. Actually the Gumbollings are ~~very~~ quite nice people. Not everyone in London is a sex-crazed criminal maniac. Unlike what they are in some other places.

The other day I had to go round to the Salmons. Scotch is off poorly. The heat makes his blood pressure rise. When

I got there he was lying on the sofa watching 'Dr Throbber's Naughty Night Nurses' and drinking Carling Black Label. Just as it got to an interesting bit, Cheyenne rushed in followed by Tara who was chasing him with an electric waffle maker. I thought they were having a bit of fun 'til Scotch grabbed the waffle maker and branded Cheyenne's head. It must have smarted because smoke came out of Cheyenne's ears and there was a terrible smell of burning. Tara was furious because her five inch heels were broken. Also because Cheyenne had put her chinchilla in the microwave. She is trying to breed them for a coat. She said at this rate she won't even get a jock strap for Scotch's Christmas present.

I tried to interest Scotch in what I had gone for (he seems to have made a big mistake on his VAT returns) but he said he was busy and turned back to 'Dr Throbber'. No wonder he's got high blood pressure. As I was leaving I saw Cheyenne and his friend, Bodger Norris, from the detention centre. They were emptying a bag of Mother's Pride on the lawn, so even if he does'nt like chinchillas, Cheyenne is kind to birds.

Kim.

Arts Centre Sculpture Exhibition

WEDNESDAY.

Dear Tracey,

No. But I've been to every museum, art gallery, theatre and cinema in London. I have now got Tutenkhamen's tomb mixed up with the Barbican Pit. Nan gets very 'agitato' whenever I go up West. She doesn't think there is life beyond the Elephant and Castle. I've got to agree most of it *is* mummified remains.

The other day Jake asked me over for a 'conference'.

When I got to his flat he was sitting cross-legged staring at the sludgy green wall and listening to 'Supertramp'. He's had his flat done up as part of his experiment. It's painted 'Estuary Green', which is sort of the colour of scum on the canal. It is dead trendy. He got the paint from an offer in the 'Observer' colour mag.

He's decided we should have a trial separation. Seeing me is interfering with his ability to experience alternative sensual options. We are not to meet for at least a fortnight while he goes on a residential to get in touch with himself.

Love,
Kim.

P.S. Thanks for the info on me mam. Has she noticed you are following her yet?

FRIDAY.

Dear Mam,

Actually I knew. Tracey told me she had seen you with him in five different places. Which is four too many to be coincidence. You say Gary has given new meaning to your life so I hope you will be very happy. What does it matter if someone has acne if they have a beautiful soul?

I cannot write any more. I have got to clean up the house before the home help arrives.

~~Love~~
Kim.

P.S. What was the *old* meaning?

Dear Tracey,

I have got to face the fact that I am the daughter of a woman with a TOYBOY! Now I will never be able to come home! You are lucky your mother died young! Trust mine to shame me up in front of everybody! I am dead choked.

Kim.

MONDAY.

Dear Mam,

I did not ask Tracey to spy on you. It is natural to be worried about your mother when you are so far away. You say it doesn't make any difference to your feelings about me and that is true. You're still criticizing everything I do. Yes I *am* still going round with Ruth. She's the only person I can talk to. Well, I talk to Nan and Marvin of course but they have limited conversation. Especially Nan. Ruth has been very understanding. She says you're having an early menopause and women often go loopy with that. I have not told Nan about 'you know who'. She already thinks you're a nymphomaniac and a murderer.

Kim.

Ruth's Kitchen

THURSDAY.

Dear Tracey,
Do not tell me any more! You'd think a middle-aged woman with an appendix scar would have more dignity than to go round pushing Gary's demo tape and telling people she's 'with the band'. My mother a *groupie!*

62

Ruth took me to a club the other night to cheer me up. It was in a portokabin under a flyover. At first I felt embarrassed as it was all women and they were dancing together and necking and that. But after a while I couldn't resist the disco. FAB. Ruth is a brill dancer but I think the six lager and blackcurrants helped. Janice didn't come with us as she is going steady with Damien or 'Raging Bull' as Ruth calls him.

By the way, I have now met two official addicts. They are Cheyenne Salmon and Bodger Norris. They were outside the club throwing stones at pigeons, or at the women when they left. Then Cheyenne put a Mother's Pride wrapper on his head (he's still got an 'H' in his No. 1 where a waffle maker hit him) and staggered about making throwing up noises. Ruth said it was the glue, it always gets you like that. She's had experience with addicts, her ex-boyfriend used to snort hair lacquer. I said should we help him but Ruth said not unless we wanted to end up like the Copydex, dripping all down his jumper. She clove-hitched him to a lamp-post with his braces and said the police could pick him up later.

Bloody Nora!
Kim.

P.S. Thank God my mother is too old to get pregnant.

FRIDAY.

Dear Jake,

Thanks for the post card. I'm really glad you are getting to grips with your carnal appetites. Does that mean you have stopped eating meat? You certainly have got an interesting group of people there. I didn't know policemen were allowed to be gay.

Yes. I am fab! Great. Fine. OK. High spot of the week

63

was unblocking the U-bend in the lavatory. The home help had put Marvin's cat litter down it. I called a 24-HOUR NEVER LET YOU DOWN INSTANT EMERGENCY PLUMBER but he was on his holidays.

I have discovered that my mother is getting some direct sensual experience. I'm still ploughing through 'War and Peace'.

Kim.

P.S. I am a bit depressed.

Ruth's room

MONDAY.

Dear Tracey,

Isn't she?!

Well I hope she is still on the pill!

Yes I am feeling better. I haven't answered my mother's last two letters. Jake has now got the wrong end of the stick. I told him I was depressed and he thinks it's because I am missing him. He keeps sending me sloppy alternative option post cards. Actually I have been having a brill time going round with Ruth.

Saturday night we went to a party at Scotch's. It was his and Tara's Silver Anniversary. Though judging by their furniture it should have been leather and marble. Tara Salmon was wearing a Designer Mexican Lamé Catsuit with chinchilla earrings and bracelet to match and even Scotch had made an effort and put his false teeth in. Tara's always been a bit off with me so I complimented her outfit. She said yes it had been made by a personal friend, though Ruth said later she had seen them in Brixton market. Come to think of it Tara might have meant the earrings. Perhaps she said made *out* of a personal friend.

They'd decorated the patio with fairy lights and fake flowers and Scotch's stuffed alsatian head had an orange in its mouth. The band were about 180 and played cha-chas and foxtrots all night. Ruth said she'd never seen a fox trot. They were always running for their lives. Scotch and Tara did the Paso Doblé to 'Hey Viva Espana'. Tara was dead Spanish with a carnation between her teeth and Scotch was very lifelike on all fours as the drunken bull. He had to move a bit sharpish to avoid her castanets.

In the break we had Pina Coladas and barbecued southern-style ribs. The drummer, who was seventy-five with a toupée and no teeth, tried to get off with Ruth but she shoved his drumstick up his nostril. Then Scotch

lurched over and told us a dirty joke. He said Ruth was a right miserable git because she did not laugh. He was dead surprised when he landed up in the fountain. I bet he has never met a girl who can shift twenty stone with one foot before.

After that we thought we better go in case he turned really nasty. On our way out through the patio we passed Cheyenne and Bodger who were barbecueing the tortoise. If I hadn't been so depressed I'd have thought it was a dead good party.

Must go now as Nan is hoovering round my feet and I am supposed to be making the home help's coffee.

All the best,
Kim.

Dear Mother,

I am sorry you find it inconvenient not to be able to ring me. Nan will not have a phone put in as she says people only ring you up in the middle of the night to say dirty things about your undies. Anyway I'm surprised you've had time to worry about me, Tracey says you have been seen out every night for a month. I quite agree about getting back to normal. Does that mean Gary has dropped you for someone more his own age?

Things are absolutely normal here.

Nan has lost the new roll-ons I bought her. She left them on the garden fence while she went to have a pee.

Irina Gumbolling has been arrested for shoplifting again. She'd been reading a review that said she danced the dying swan like an ageing pig in labour. They found her wandering in Marks with a pair of 'Y' fronts in her bag. She is obviously trying to tell Gordon something.

I've had to replace Mr Bibby's window boxes twice this week. The first time the dustmen snatched his geraniums. But who on earth managed to get away with a three foot barrel as well as the hydrangea in it I cannot imagine.

Mrs Webster has finally done it. Janice told her she and Damien were getting engaged and she went straight out and threw herself off the balcony. Fortunately her moon boot got caught in the railings so she didn't fall. But she dangled there for ages before anybody noticed.

Summer is nearly over. I've been on the gardening scheme for six months and I haven't been supervised once. I don't know what I will do when it comes to an end. I could manage on my wages at Scotch's except I never get them. No wonder his books are in such a mess. He has taken me off them now. He said he didn't pay me to be nosy. I said he didn't pay me at all but he picked up a spanner and looked menacing.

Kim.

Mrs V. Pretty,
'Paws'
Pett Corner,
Clapham

Dear Mrs Pretty,

I saw your ad. for a pet shop assistant in our local corner shop and I'd like to apply for the job.

I have had lots of experience with Pets, Budgies, Dogs and Cats especially and am fond of all animals. Except spiders. They make me scream. I once would not have a bath for a week because one had got trapped in the plug-hole. So *NO* spiders.

Sorry about that. I heard a sudden yowling outside and rushed to see what it was. It was Marvin (my cat) who had got next-door-but-one's tabby trapped up a tree. Ruth (my friend) had to climb up and get her. I have given her some Good Girl drops to calm her down (the tabby not Ruth) and shut Marvin in the scullery without his tea. My Nan says animals respond to a firm hand.

When would it be convenient to start?

Yours affectionately,
Kim Kirby.

Dear Mother,

I didn't mean to sound 'down' in my letter. Things could be worse. I could be in a wheelchair like Mrs Webster, or pregnant like Janice or in prison like Irina. I am only jobless, penniless and nearly an orphan.

I have just finished scrubbing out the scullery. Nan told the home help not to come any more. She said she couldn't afford the coffee, tea and biscuits. Now I've got to go and get Nan's fags, *she* is sitting with Marvin on her lap. She's stolen his affections. She thinks he loves her for herself but actually it's for the chicken supreme with chunky bits. She says he is very intelligent and understands everything she says. I said in that case why didn't she send *him* out for the fags?

~~Depressed,~~
Kim.

Dear Tracey,

Jake has decided we can have sex. He has asked me to get a blood test?!

Kim.

Dear Gary,

Thank you for your note.

I don't know why my mother thinks it would be better if we had some personal contact. The last time we had any was when you trapped my plaits in Barry Gummer's bicycle wheel. Still, it is nice to know that you 'genuinely' care about my mother and have fancied older women ever since you saw Marilyn Monroe in 'The Seven Year Itch'. I cannot see much similarity between Marilyn Monroe and my mother except for the time she caught scabies but of course I haven't seen her since she dyed her hair blonde.

I have played your demo tape to Jake (my boyfriend). He said it was 'post punk heavy metal with a sub-text of Iron Maiden'. My friend Ruth said it was bollocks.

Tell my mother to stop worrying about me. I am not going to take an overdose. Dr Cadoza wouldn't give me any sleeping pills.

Yours sincerely,
Kim.

P.S. Ruth meant what Jake said was bollocks, not your tape. Anyway you don't have to take any notice of her, she only likes rappin and dub.

Dear Tracey,

The Aids leaflet has just come through our door. Nan picked it up and said was it from the Jehovah's Witnesses? I snatched it off her before she had time to read it though. I don't want an angina attack on my hands.

Later.

I have just finished reading it. Blimey. I'm going straight out to ring Jake up and say it is all off. Don't touch Nigel's unless you boil it first in Dettol and wear two pairs of rubber gloves!

> Yours in chastity,
> Kim.

THURSDAY.

Dear Mam,

Thank you for the photo. Gary *has* got long hair. Is that a tattoo on his nose or a boil? *You* look like I remember you when I was little. It made me feel quite funny. I showed it to Nan (I cut Gary's bit off first of course) and she said she'd never seen you look so young and happy. Not even when you were first married. I did not tell her what you said about your honeymoon.

Please thank Gary for his letter. It *was* nice of him to write. Tell him I have played his tape again and really quite like it. Nan said it sounded like a pack of wolves howling so that is a good sign.

No, Irina is out. She got off with a fine and a warning. Her solicitor said it was 'that time of the month'. Mrs Webster is getting better too. She did have a bit of a setback when Janice let go of the wheelchair as she was pushing her downstairs (the lift is still out of order) but she was wearing a padded ski suit so luckily she bounced. Yes, Janice *is* pregnant, Ruth says she's a ~~ratbrat~~ stupid cow, but Janice says she's always wanted a dear little baby of her own.

Thanks for the money. Seen! It's in the nick of time as Nan and me are going on an outing with St Agnes Community Centre. It's hop picking in Kent. Nan says she hopes Mr Bibby doesn't come as last time he got pissed as a fart.

Kim.

P.S. By the way. Has Gary read that leaflet on Aids?

FRIDAY.

Dear Tracey,

I've just got back from seeing Jake and am absolutely wild! He said where had I been the last six months, everyone knew about Aids. I was so ignorant, etc. etc. why did I think he'd asked me to take a blood test? Bloody cheek!!! I was that mad I ripped me cap out (I'd put it in just in case, it took me an hour and a half and Nan's darning mushroom) and dropped it in his herbal tea.

No wonder he was blathering on about 'alternative sensual adventures' he was dead scared of catching owt! Well that's *it*! I am finishing with him. It's just as well. I'm sick of bloody high fibre. I've been going to the lav three times a day and Nan is complaining about the waste of paper. She says she made do with one roll a fortnight and 'The Sun' torn into strips before I came to stay.

Yours in disgust,
Kim.

Dear Gary,

Yes I think this demo is better. Who is that making the peculiar wailing noise in the background?

    Seen.

Kim.

Bingo (Not me. Waiting for Nan).

FRIDAY.

Dear Mam,

Not *peculiar* exactly more . . . *different*. You *are* taking singing seriously aren't you.

    I was only repeating what Nan said about Mr Bibby. I don't know why it shocked you. It used to be Gary's favourite expression. Anyway she was quite right. It started out OK. It was a really brill day. You could smell it was nearly Autumn but it was bright and warm. We all got the coach at the community centre. It took ages to get on it. Mrs Salmon had to be pushed up the stairs by four people. We'd just got a decent seat when Nan decided she had to go to the lav. Mr Bibby asked her if she was wearing her green or her pink, which made her very suspicious. As soon as we got going Mr Bibby fetched the brown ale out. Nan and Mrs Salmon ignored him but the vicar had a bottle. After a while everyone started to sing. Songs from the first world war, Nan said. She kept joining in and then stopping to wipe her eyes. By the time we got there everyone had had a good cry.

    The place was really great. It was a little old-fashioned hop house with a picking and drying shed. Everybody got behind a bin and started hopping away with a break every three minutes for a cup of tea and a cheese and pickle sandwich. After lunch we didn't see Mr Bibby again until it was time to go. The local pub was having a real ale festival. Personally I don't think I'd have paid the hoppers in beer tokens.

When we got back on the bus Mr Bibby was reeling. He sang a hymn to Mrs Salmon and tried to kiss the vicar. Nan had had quite a few as well by that time. She hit Mr Bibby with her souvenir hop bin and he slumped to his knees and then passed out. Everyone snoozed for a bit and then Mr Bibby woke up and started talking about his ~~sex life~~ war time experiences. He said he used to have ten or twelve a week and still expected to have at least one. He then made up a song about the day out. Nan said it was disgusting but the vicar joined in.

Nan was shattered by the time we got home. I had her leaning on one side of me and Mr Bibby on the other all the way from the centre. It was a bit awkward as they refused to speak to each other. They won't get another outing for ages. St Agnes has had its grant cut and they can't afford to keep the community bus. I've mended the engine a few times for nothing but I wish I could do something more to help. The vicar has put out an appeal for funds but so far all he's received is hate mail. Most of it from the Council.

Love,
Kim.

73

Dear Gary,

How about setting this to music? The lyrics are rather similar to your last demo.

> I'm coming up behind you
> I'm going to make you scream
> I'll tickle you 'til you're jelly
> I'll grab at your ice cream
> I want to hold and squeeze you
> Let you bite my stick of rock
> Gobble up your candy floss
> Put toffee in your sock
>
> Oh Sugar lick my lolly
> Lick my lolly
> All night long
> Oh Sugar lick my lolly
> And I'll sing you my song.
>   (Harold Bibby '87)

SATURDAY.

Dear Jake,

I am afraid I am busy on Monday. I am starting a course in car maintenance at an adult institution. You cannot come and meet me there as it is women only.

Yours faithfully,
Kim.

WEDNESDAY.

Dear Tracey,

I am sticking to it even though I've had two begging letters from Jake. How about you? Did Nigel agree to wait until you are married?

74

Actually I've heard even married people can get it. The other day I was at the Gumbollings' cutting off red hot pokers when I heard shouting coming from the bathroom. I expected something to come crashing through the window as usual so I ducked just in time to miss the sink. Later I asked Irina what was wrong. She said she had got thrushes. I said I couldn't see anything wrong with that, they eat slugs and have lovely voices. She said this was a fungus and it grew somewhere private. (Actually I had noticed her scratching quite a lot.) I asked her where she'd got it from and she laughed bitterly and said 'Ask Gordon. Men ought to come with a government health warning!' Gordon said she was full of rancorous man-hatred.

Janice is getting married in a fortnight. I wonder if I should tell her?

Kim.

Nan's armchair

THURSDAY.

Dear Mam,

Jake said the lyrics had 'great emotional impact and pierced straight to the aching dilemma of the pre-tumescent male' which is moreorless the same as Gary saying they had a lot of 'balls'. As for me 'coming round' to him. I could never come round to someone who wears platform shoes so let's just not talk about it. I cannot afford to come home for a few weeks yet and by then I'm sure it will all have blown over.

Talking of blowing over there's a bit of a cloud at Scotch Salmon's. The other day I was under one of his cars checking for oil leaks from the engine, I won't bother you with details, but on that sort of car you could get leakage from the sump ring, drain plug, oil filter, flange joint, cylinder block, distributor drive, pulley seal or gasket, (did I mention I had started going to car maintenance classes?) when I saw two pairs of shoes that were not Tara Salmon's five inch sling backs or Cheyenne's steel capped Doc Martin's walking up to me. It turned out they were two blokes from the VAT. They asked me to see the books and when I said they were locked up and Scotch kept the key on a bicycle chain round his neck, they turned quite nasty. They ransacked the office and were just carrying out the filing cabinet with the padlock on it when Scotch arrived back from the pub. He went wild. He threw one of the blokes into a stripping down tank and sprayed the other with T-Cut. Then he shoved his Tory party card up their noses and said was this what you got for being faithful all your life, thugs coming round to intimidate you at work? If they weren't careful he'd set Norman Tebbit on them. They did go a bit white at that.

I helped to hose them down and made them a cup of tea. But they said they would be back next week. Scotch is blaming me.

Mrs Salmon has just come round to collect Nan for their Social Sequence Dance Class. I offered to go round with them as it's after curfew time in Lambeth, but Nan said no, she wasn't going to be stopped from walking in the streets she had lived in from a child. She is wearing a crash helmet, Grandad's bicycle clips and Rover's dog lead round her waist. I only hope the police don't stop her or she'll be done for being a dangerous weapon.

Kim.

Later.

Nan has just got in so I have made us a cup of cocoa. She said she will never dance with Mrs Salmon again, she was always trying to lead. Mr Bibby spent most of the night on

76

his hands and knees. I said I supposed he was drunk again but she said no, it was a better position for looking up people's skirts when they twirled in the 'Veleta'.

Dear Tracey,

No, I'm not having a bridesmaid's frock. It is registry office. Besides it would look daft with a Mohican. I am going to spray me head pink though and I've got some day-glo laces for me Doc Martin's.

Ruth has refused to go. She and Janice haven't spoken since Ruth said any child of Damien's would be born with at least two heads.

Love,
Kim.

Dear Jake,

I do not know what you mean by a 'state of the art' relationship. But if it's anything to do with Rodin the answer is definitely no.

Yours sincerely,
Kim.

Dear Mam,

Shock Horror! Mr Bibby is dead!

Nan saw the ambulance when she went out to collect her pension. She went across as she is dead ~~nosy~~ neighbourly

and the District Nurse told her he'd had a heart attack. It happened when she called to give him his three monthly bath. She was bending over to test the water and the next thing she knew Mr Bibby was clutching her calf and making horrible choking noises. I've often wondered why they let nurses wear those black seamed stockings.

He might have pulled through if the ambulance had been quick but the nearest hospital was closed last year and the other is at least three traffic jams away. Poor old Bibby. Still at least he went out in his favourite position. Nan was dead upset. I pointed out that she hadn't liked him much in life, but she said that didn't matter, he was the last of 'her kind'. Now she is living in a street full of social workers.

Kim.

Harry Lord,
Royal Hotel,
Queen Street.

Dear Sir Harry,

I am answering your advert for a 'Junior Soup Chef'. (By the way I think I ought to let you know that the paper spelt it wrong . . . they had it printed as SOUS chef, you should try and get a rebate.) I have had a lot of experience in soup given that it is my Nan's favourite food and also very cheap. Last week I got some old bones from the butcher and boiled them up with onions and potatoes, Seen! It was meant for Marvin (our cat) but it smelt so good Nan and I ate it for our supper (we gave Marvin some of course). Heinz Tomato is still my favourite though, as it is most people's *I* think.

> Best wishes,
> Kim Kirby.

Mr Raj. Puri,
Wright Recreation Centre,
Mussel Mount,
Lambeth.

Dear Mr Puri,

I am writing on behalf of me and a friend to apply for the shared job of Ethnic Female Sports Leader for Women Only Classes.

I am not ethnic (unless you count Scottish, Welsh and Irish on my mother's side) but my friend Ruth is. Although she was born in Wandsworth her parents are from Pigs Head Bay.

I have had no training except what Ruth has given me, she often catches me with a Ju-Jitsu throw in the middle of the shopping precinct, but Ruth is ace at it. Last week she took on two muggers and a knife with her bare hands and made a citizen's arrest. Everyone round here respects her, especially the two girls she arrested.

She can speak Patois and I am learning Hindi at our local community centre.

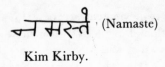 (Namaste)

Kim Kirby.

The Jolly Cockney (*Out*side waiting for Nan)

WEDNESDAY.

Dear Mam,

It was Mr Bibby's funeral today. Nan and I went out of respect. The vicar said he was an erect and active member of the community. Nan said that was certainly true. He was cremated. I put his gnome on the coffin along with the floral tributes, it's the nearest to a garden it will ever get.

Nan was quite tearful, especially at the reading of the will. Mr Bibby has left her his window boxes. His nephew also asked her if she would have any use for sixteen pairs of pink and green interlock knickers and an OS rubber roll-on.

Yes, that is the end of the job. But it was coming to an end anyway. Some bright spark has told the council there is not a blade of grass or a fallen leaf this side of Clapham Common.

I am still going to the Gumbollings' of course. Though I hardly have time to garden. Last week I did Irina's washing, ironing and shopping as well as taking Douarnier Rousseau for his walk. She is scared to go outside in case she starts nicking again. I even had to go and buy her undies. Six pairs of bikini see-through lace with 'Men Only' on a heart in the middle. I cannot imagine why she wanted

80

size XL. She's so thin she'd slip down the crazy paving if it wasn't for her thick ankles.

> Love,
> Kim.

P.S. I have just remembered why.

Dear Tracey,

The something old is Nan's nets, I have made her a head dress out of them, something new is a crucifix from her mam, something borrowed is Ruth's book on self defence and something blue a porn mag from Errol.

I am feeling quite nervous. The last wedding I went to was me mam and dad's. I didn't have to dress for that one as I was inside her.

Errol is best man. He is giving Janice a lift to the service on his bike. He said as it was only a hundred yards he didn't mind but he's not going out if it's raining.

> Wish me luck,
> Kim.

Bed.

Dear Tracey,

It was absolutely ace. It was a really sunny day and I got round to the Tower dead early which was just as well as Errol was so busy fixing CB aerials to his bike that he hadn't noticed his front wheel nut was loose. If he'd had to turn a corner he would have killed them both.

81

I got that fixed then went up to collect Janice and Conan who had a new pink muzzle for the occasion. Janice was in a terrible state. Her mum and dad had had a row. Her mother had thrown a slice of bacon at her dad and her dad had thrown the cooker off the balcony. He was now threatening to throw Janice's mam after it and she was begging him to hurry up. Janice was clinging on to her mother's bandaged leg and everyone was screaming. Remembering Ruth's advice I threw a bucket of cold water over them and locked Mr Webster in the bathroom when he went to get a towel.

The rest of it passed off without bother. Errol forgot the ring but fortunately I had one in my nose and Damien had a bit of bother with the answers as he cannot read.

Ruth was outside. She showered me and Janice with confetti but ignored Damien completely. Errol said it looked like Janice had married me. Janice was almost fainting with happiness. In fact as soon as we got back to the flat she went straight to the lav and was sick.

The reception was fab. Me and Janice had done the food the night before. Nan wouldn't touch it. She said the first bite had finished her. Later Ruth found her dentures in the cheese and celery dip. Me and Ruth got completely pissed on Asti Spumante. So did Mrs Webster. She started to strip after her third glass while Mr Webster did a slow hand clap. I've never seen them being nice to each other before.

Janice and Damien disappeared for ages. I think they were doing 'you know what'. Ruth said they were wasting their time. Damien would never get it in the right way round more than once and Janice would not be much help, she still thought babies came out of your navel.

At last they came out in their going away gear. Janice had a frock like Fergie's she bought in C & A and Damien had a lurex jacket. It seemed a bit over the top as they were only going to spend the night at the swimming pool. Damien was on duty.

Me and Ruth went down to the centre after. There was a new rapper. She was F.A.B. Jake was there. He sent a message across that he wanted a 'counselling' session, but I told him to get stuffed.

Kim.

TUESDAY.

Dear Mam,

Mrs Webster has moved out of her room for Janice and Damien. She said she didn't have any use for the double bed now as Mr Webster only comes home about once a month and then he is too pissed to bother. He usually passes out in the lift and spends the night there. Mrs Webster is sleeping on the sofa with the handlebars of Errol's bike.

Irina and Gordon have also moved into separate rooms. Gordon sits up in bed 'til four or five in the morning typing out bits of his novel. Irina asked me if I thought it was grounds for divorce.

Tara Salmon has asked Scotch for a divorce. Cheyenne is dead pleased. He said next time he gets nicked he can tell the judge he's the child of a broken marriage and get everybody sobbing.

Love,
Kim.

P.S. Forgot to say Janice and Damien got married on Saturday.

Dear Tracey,

Do you think bringing the wedding forward is a good idea?
Even if Nigel does say he will go sterile if he has to stop
short any longer. Ruth says to buy him a jock strap.

I did go and see Jake in the end. He said he couldn't
discharge his workload with emotional stress on his mind.
Ruth said she'd seen him at the centre and he wasn't too
upset to discharge several pints of bitter. But I gave in. He
has now drawn us up a contract.

1) We will see each other twice a week on a 'non-coital'
   basis.
2) I will read the following books
   'Lady Chatterley's Lover'
   'The Joy of Sex'
   'The Art of Loving'
   'Sensual Massage'
   'Rolfing and Golfing'
   'Adventures with Alexander'
   'Freud and Feeling'
3) *He* will take a blood test.

Kim!

P.S. I have started 'Lady Chatterley's Lover'. It is not the
sort of thing you would want your mother to read.

P.P.S. I wonder if my mother *was* reading it when she met
Gary Prescott?

Dear Mam,

Yes, you and Gary are the only couple I know who are still
going strong. Except for Janice and Damien of course.

Janice did have a black eye on Saturday but she said she trod on the shag pile rake.

It's kind of Gary to offer to decorate my room. Actually I like it the way it is. I do not want to come home at Christmas and find my ivy patterned wallpaper replaced by Tommy the Tank.

I am desperately trying to save up for presents but Scotch hasn't paid me for a month. Tara is divorcing him because he won't buy her a new en suite bathroom with two speed bidet and avocado whirlpool. It is all because of the VAT. The men came back with a security van and totally cleared the office. Scotch is hopping as the filing cabinet was full of Glen Morangie.

Later.

Nan has just been looking at 'Crimewatch' (her favourite after Three Two One) and she saw a stolen car that is the dead spit of Scotch's. Raunchy red with a bunch of banana exhaust and a sticker on the window saying 'Married Men Make Better Lovers'. It was stolen from the Rotary Club the week that Scotch employed me. I wonder if he realizes he's driving a stolen car? I'm not going to be the one to tell him, it's too near Christmas to risk a broken limb. Nan said she'd have a word with Mrs Salmon next time she goes to whist.

Kim.

TUESDAY.

Dear Tracey,

Don't breathe a word to me mam but I have found out my employer is a car thief!

I don't know what to do as I have been threatened that if I 'grass' Cheyenne and Bodger Norris will pay me a visit. Bodger is six foot four tall and four feet six wide and has already been on probation for hitting a Chelsea fan with a pillar box (he is a Crystal Palace supporter). I am scared to go out of the house in case he's waiting to brain me with a lamp post. I've had to tell Nan I have got the 'flu and now she is panicking and saying it is Aids. Fat chance!

Yours in terror,
Kim.

WEDNESDAY.

Dear Mam,

False alarm! Nan asked Mrs Salmon about the car and Mrs Salmon asked Scotch and Scotch came round and explained that the car he drives is a *green* E-Type. I must be colour blind.

He took me outside for a chat and sure enough there was an E-Type in British racing green with silver go-fast strips on its side. It didn't have a bunch of banana exhaust any longer either.

Kim.

THURSDAY.

Dear Tracey,

The heat is off.

So is the job. I have been sacked for being colour blind. I've also been banned from the premises and threatened that if I say a word to the VAT men I will end up in the boot of a very crushed Cortina.

I am fed up of London. The Gumbollings are the only thing between me and starvation. Thank God it's nearly Christmas. Jake has offered to lend me the fare home if I can't get a job in time. His blood test was negative but I don't want to be beholden. Irina is paying me to do her Christmas shopping though, so I might save up enough.

Christmas cheer, etc.
Kim.

Des DareDevil Despatches,
Speed Street,
W.1.

FRIDAY.

Dear Des,

I'd like to become a DareDevil Despatcher.

I haven't got a motor bike at present but I have done a deal with my friend Errol. I can borrow his if I give him all my back copies of the Beano and 80% of my earnings. Fair enough.

Yours daringly,
KiKi.

P.S. Do I have to learn tricks?

MONDAY.

Dear Mam,

What do you mean it is too late he has already done it it is a lovely shade of chocolate? *Chocolate!* It's a bloody good job I *am* colour blind.

No I have not found another job. I spent all day up West looking. I was offered handing out leaflets for a hairdresser but they said I'd have to have my own styled first as I wasn't a good advertisement. I said thanks but I didn't want a leopard spotted Afro or my head and eyebrows shaved. Nan will not get her set of hang gliding lessons at this rate.

Kim.

Dear Mother,

I will say bloody if I want to. I am nearly eighteen. I'm fed up with you treating me as though I am a kid. Do you tell Gary Prescott to wear a vest and not to talk to strangers?

London is a bloody nightmare. I have been doing Irina's bloody Christmas shopping. I nearly got my bloody eye poked out in Harrods. Some bloody woman was after the same bloody tin of snails' eggs. Coming home on the tube was bloody awful. There were four bloody headlines opposite me – 'Nuclear Crash. Bloody Disaster', 'Bloody Headless Corpse in Wood', 'Jobless Total Bloody Four Million', 'Bloody Baby Dies of Aids'. At least nobody tries to feel you up any more, they are all too bloody scared of catching it.

There was a bit of a hold-up at bloody Bank, some bloody body had thrown themselves on the line.

Bloody Kim.

P.S. I expect Nan *will* break her bloody neck. The vicar is giving the lessons from St Agnes's bloody clock tower.

Thursday

Dear Mam,
    I am ~~bloody~~ sorry. I was a bit upset that day. It was what you said in your letter about Gary moving in. No wonder he was painting my bedroom. You haven't let him see Teddy have you? I'll never forgive you if you do!

Kim!

Mrs Kirby
Lakeland
Wordsworth Walk
off London road

MONDAY.

Dear Mam,

Cross. Of course I'm cross. How would you feel if I told you I was going to live with Gordon Gumbolling?! Does Gary's mother know what's going on? I can't write any more, I am late for my car maintenance class. If I don't turn up in time the instructor will top herself with carbon monoxide fumes. Out of fourteen women I am the only one still going.

Kim.

P.S. Dusty will leave home. She doesn't get on with strangers.

89

Dear Tracey,

Bloody Gary Prescott has moved in with me mam! She says it is a 'temporary measure while he looks around for digs'. He was thrown out of his last lot for keeping rabbits' blood in the deep freeze. I don't know what she means by 'temporary' but if he's still there at Christmas I will not be coming home.

I have been dead depressed. It's funny but I really miss Scotch Salmon and Mr Bibby. At least it was something to do all day.

Nan and I have had a terrible row. She got furious when I said St Agnes's should be used for dossers. After all there are only sixteen people in the congregation unless you count the pigeons that are nesting in the roof.

I said Jesus was kind to the poor and she said it was different in his country, the poor didn't drink methylated spirits. She couldn't see the vicar on his hands and knees cleaning up the vomit. I said it wasn't their fault. The government had driven them to live like that. She said they were a load of workshy moaning minnies and thank goodness we had a government who weren't afraid to say so, they should all be rounded up and given voluntary euthanasia. I asked her if she included me in that as I was out of a job. She said no at least I was trying. I should give it a year before committing suicide. I said I had nearly thrown myself under a number 77. She said be sure not to do it in the rush hour as it was very inconvenient.

I was so angry I called her an effing hypocrite. I said how could she call herself a Christian when she had views like that? She said God helps those who help themselves. I said God was a Tory in that case and she said yes. Then I refused to help her to fill in her application for BA shares. That really got her mad. It is her ambition to be the first nonegenarian to own a Concorde sickbag. We are still not speaking.

Kim.

FRIDAY.

Dear Mam,

No I am *not* going to live with Gordon Gumbolling. Not now I have seen him with the 'flu. It is lucky Mrs Prescott is so broad-minded. She is probably glad to get Gary off her hands. Especially if she doesn't have a deep freeze.

I have got a job. It's doing market research for a double glazing company.

Later.

I *had* a job. After eight hours in the freezing cold I have been kicked, used as a chewing gum post and peed on by a dog. Only one person stopped to do my questionnaire. She was an OAP who felt sorry for me. I told her double glazing was investing in her future. She said 'I'm eighty seven dearie, I haven't got a future'. Tara Salmon walked by on the other side of the road and pretended not to see me.

 ~~Bloody~~ Nora
Kim.

SUNDAY.

Dear Tracey,

You can't be serious. You really agree with Nan? I don't see what the Prime Minister looking better now she's had her teeth done has got to do with it! Ruth says it's an official secret where she gets her youthful looks. Her last hairdresser had his salon ransacked when he breathed the words 'Glo-Curl For That Color Confidence'.

Saw Cheyenne in the dole queue today. He didn't even make a threatening gesture. He did clutch at a chair as though he was going to throw it but fortunately he couldn't as it was screwed to the floor. I even miss Cheyenne I have been so bored.

Of course I have been seeing Jake. I know he's a pillock but he's dead good looking. Anyway you can talk, you finished with Nigel three times before you got engaged. I don't know if I fancy Jake any more. All the problems of sex seem to get in the way of enjoying it. Do you still fancy Nigel?

Janice is wild for Damien. She is always trying to get him to do it. Ruth says she is obsessed and it's not normal for a married couple. Mrs Webster got very upset when she found them on the kitchen table. She said she wouldn't have minded so much but they'd rolled all over her shepherd's pie. Another time they were hanging over the balcony. Janice had her legs round Damien's waist and Damien had his hands round Janice's neck. Mrs Webster said it was like history repeating itself. She has banned them from everywhere but the bedroom.

I'm going for a job at a supermarket tomorrow. They take on extra staff at Christmas and I can get a discount on Marvin's catfood. Nan grumbles that he's better fed than any of us, but she couldn't stop me giving him my sausages today as she's still not speaking to me.

Kim.

P.S. No, he doesn't *drink* the blood. He uses it in his stage act.

Dear Mam,

Please tell Gary to stop writing to me to tell me how upset you are. Personally I cannot see what you have got to be upset about. You have got a house, a cat and a boyfriend. The cat is very nice. I am *not* punishing you.

I cannot come home for Christmas. Sleeping on the sofa just wouldn't be the same.

I had an interview at Sharpe's supermarket yesterday. I can have a part time evening job 'til Christmas as long as the overall fits and I promise to wear a hat. The wages are rotten.

Kim.

The hairdresser's.

MONDAY.

Dear Tracey,

Your letter was very interesting. You mean you've *never* fancied Nigel? Have you faced the fact that for the next fifty years you're going to have to close your eyes and think about Simon Le Bon? Ruth says you are barking.

Jake and I had another tussle on Saturday. This time it was *me* trying to get *him* not to be scared of passion. We'd been to see 'Prick Up Your Ears' and I was really randy. I put the gas logfire to 'glow' and lit a couple of candles. I even took one of me Doc Martin's off so he could get me tights past me knees but it was no good he just couldn't do it. He said it was the beer but he'd only had half a pint. It was dead embarrassing rolling about with this limp thing flopping from side to side. Perhaps there's something wrong with me? I asked Ruth but she just said 'Don't worry, you're friggin' gorgeous'.

Janice and Damien are still going strong. He may be a
rubber-headed hulk (Ruth's description) but at least he can
get it on. Mrs Webster wears permanent ear muffs to drown
out the noise. On Sunday she barricaded them out of the
flat so she could have her lie-in. They went to get the
caretaker to break down the door but he wouldn't come out
as his German shepherd was in bed bad with nerves. He
said it was more than his life was worth to patrol the estate
alone. In the end they came round and asked me if they
could borrow a bed. Fortunately Nan was out at church so
I lent them the put-u-up sofa. Then Marvin and I went
into the kitchen and shut the door. It was deafening.
Especially as Marvin joined in. I cannot bear to think of
my mother doing that with Gary Prescott!

Kim

Dear Mam,

I do not care if Gary moves into the *chimney*, I am not coming home for Christmas!

Started my new job at Sharpe's last night. It was more like a casualty department than a supermarket. The girl who showed me the till had her arm in a sling and her feet in a plastic bag. Before she left she pressed a box of pills into my hand and said 'You'll need these, you're on the suicide shift'. It's mind-bogglingly boring. The till is all computerized so you don't even have to add up. I hadn't been there half an hour when the first fight broke out. Two Clapham trendies nipping each other's ankles with their trolleys. Neither would let the other go first in the queue. Then there was a scuffle over the last jar of mock caviar. An OAP with a walking frame won.

The hours dragged by. I soon discovered what the plastic bag was for. Your feet get frozen and you can't move your legs. I'm still not sure about the sling though.

Love,
Kim.

p.s. Would you like a Nutri-Bran Muesli pudding for Christmas?

Sharpe's (Till 14)

MONDAY.

Dear Tracey,

Jake has got 'anxiety related impotence'! Dr Dickey said not to worry it is very common but there are no known figures as most men don't report it. Jake reckons it's because we waited so long that now he can't do it. So it *is* my fault after all! We have got to have lots of sensual massage sessions so I am skipping through the book.

I also had a long talk with Irina Gumbolling when I took her the rubber catalogue she has bought Gordon for Christmas. Her friend Dulcima Gatsby was there and they were drinking Lapsang Souchong and eating chocolate biscuits. Well, Dulcima was eating chocolate biscuits. Irina has to sick up everything she eats so she usually doesn't bother. Dulcima grabbed the catalogue and shrieked at all the pictures. After she had finished she demanded an explanation. Well then it all came out. Irina cried and said she had never had an 'organism'. Dulcima said she hadn't had one that week and ate another biscuit. Next thing I knew I was talking about my mother. Dulcima said lucky her, she wouldn't mind some 'teenbait'. Irina said I mustn't begrudge her some pleasure, women got little enough Dulcima said she could speak for herself there were ways of getting your kicks (she is an adjudicator for Greek dancing) and Irina said nothing compared with good sex with someone you were in love with. Or so she'd heard.

I was amazed. To think these old crumblies are still going on about sex. There is obviously something to it I haven't discovered yet. I must admit it got me thinking about me mam. Supposing *she's* never had an organism? No wonder she went funny in the head and talked to herself all the time. She could end up an absolute loony like Irina. Maybe Gary Prescott is doing us all a favour!

K!

Dear Mam,

Please find enclosed 'The Joy of Sex' as part of your Christmas present.

I went into work tonight but found we were all on strike. Alex, the shop steward, had called it because of the overtime pay. That is because of the *lack* of the overtime pay. Alex was standing on a soap box (Persil Automatic) making a speech. He said the ruthless employer was exploiting the under twenty-ones and he pointed at me. I tried to hide behind the baked bean mountain but he carried on talking about the 'infamous act' and the 'living in' system. I didn't understand a word of it but later while everyone was standing around smoking fags and talking about their Christmas shopping he got hold of me and explained that there is a new wages bill that doesn't limit hours of work or time off or anything. It's specially bad for young people who are desperate for work. He said that as the youngest member to join I'd been elected to demand festive overtime from the management. I said I hadn't joined, at which point he whipped out a form.

Everybody clapped and the next thing I knew I was on my way to ask the ruthless employer for a rise. By this time there was a huge queue of people outside the shop. They were shouting and banging on the window and everybody inside was giving them the V-sign. Stella Shaw was dead flustered. She said she couldn't take the decision herself but she'd put it to the management board. In the meantime if we would get back to work before the riot police arrived she'd give us a special bonus.

Everybody cheered when I came back and Alex presented me with a bottle of pink champagne from the booze counter. We toasted the crowd and wished them Merry Christmas while they clawed at the glass and pulled horrible faces. I don't feel such a stranger now. Beverley (on the till next door) has lent me her hot water bottle.

Kim.

97

MONDAY.

Dear Tracey,

Alex, the shop steward has asked me for a date. I don't know what to do. I don't like the idea of two-timing, but if I finish with Jake now he will think it's because of the sex! By the way, it is 'orgasm' not 'organism' Ruth told me. I asked her if she had had one and she laughed and said three or four a night depending on her partner.

I have told Alex he can escort me to the Sharpe's Christmas party.

Kim.

P.S. It is not 'posh' to say Lapsang Souchong. Gordon Gumbolling says wilful ignorance is the scourge of the working class.

P.P.S. Actually *I* used to think it was a Pekinese dog.

THURSDAY.

Dear Mam,

For the last time *no*. Nan has bought a chicken and everything. She says it's the first time since she got married she's had company for Christmas.

Yes I am still at Sharpe's. What do you mean 'if my card gets marked Union Activist I will never get a job'? I was not being a 'Union Activist'. I was just asking for what we deserved. The special bonus was a hamper of Christmas goodies so Nan and I will be alright. She'll have to do the cooking though as I now have my arm in a sling.

I've been invited to three Christmas parties, Sharpe's,

Ruth's and Irina Gumbolling's. Nan's going to nineteen if you count St Agnes's wake for the Martyrs.

                                                                Kim.

P.S. You didn't mention what you thought of your Christmas present.

Merry Xmas

Happy Christmas!
Does this cat remind you of
anybody?
(The record token is for you both.
It'll make a change from Gary's
tapes).

← paw print from Marvin
   to Dusty
xxxxxxx

Dear Trace,

Thanks for the card. I've had four, if you count the post card from Scotch and Tara Salmon. They've gone on a make up holiday to the Seychelles so they must be feeling generous (not generous enough to pay my back wages though).

I have had a sensual massage session with Jake. It was a bit awkward with one arm in a sling (I've got a touch of tendonitis) but we managed alright. Actually I really liked it. Where did Nigel read that it's normal for women not to have orgasms?

Your party frock sounds nice. See through's all the rage this year. It's Sharpe's Do tonight! I am wearing Ruth's leather skirt and my new second-hand down-to-the-ground man's overcoat. F.A.B.

Merry Christmas,
Kim. x

Christmas Eve

Dear Mam,

Sorry about the panic phone call, I was in a state of shock. I've just got back from the hospital and they think she's going to be fine. Well OK. Obviously it is a terrible blow to come in from a party and find your house completely ransacked. It's lucky she was drunk or the angina attack might have been worse.

The police came to the hospital to interview Nan. She said she came in to the kitchen and saw the cupboards hanging open and the carving knife ready on the table. Her first thought was for Marvin but he was fast asleep in her knitting bag as usual. After that she just collapsed and that was how I found her. The policemen were very kind. One of them said he would say a prayer for Nan and the other said he would ask his voices for guidance. They have been round to take away the carving knife. It's no use to us as the burglars stole the chicken. Also the stuffing, the sprouts and the sherry trifle. I'm going to Ruth's for Christmas lunch.

The hospital are keeping Nan in for a few days' observation. At least there she'll be warm and able to watch Terry

100

Wogan (we no longer have a fire or a telly) but of course I can't possibly come home now until she's better, so forget New Year. She looked very old and little propped up in the hospital bed.

I will post this now although I know you won't get it 'til after Christmas so have a lovely time and give Dusty my special cuddle.

Don't worry about me. Several people have offered me a bed.

Lots of love,
Kim.

The Hospital

CHRISTMAS WEEK

Dear Trace,

Me mam told you all about it then. Nan is snoozing on her bed pan so I'll just dash off a few lines. I've had an amazing time. It's been like one long party. It started with Sharpe's which went on till 2 A.M. Alex is fab. He is a great dancer and really makes me laugh even when he talks about politics. He is also a great kisser as I found out at 2.30 am. When I got in me Nan was lying on the kitchen floor. At first I thought she was dead, especially when I saw the carving knife on the table. But she came round when I breathed on her and said she'd have a small port. The ambulance took ages as they'd had a Christmas rush but she's alright now and definitely on the mend.

I went to Ruth's for Christmas lunch which was Ace. We had chicken and rice and peas and okra and plantain and sweet potato and yam. I had four Special Brews and Ruth had six. Clovis and Selvin could only manage three. After dinner while Mr and Mrs Baptiste watched the Queen's speech her sister Hanna entertained us with a dance drama. It was a kung fu ballet she had learned at school entitled 'Growing up in Brixton'. That night the rest of the family came and we partied until breakfast. It's amazing how many people you can get into one front room. We had soul music and soul food and even the walls were moving!

Talking of moving Nan is making grunting noises so I'd better stop. I'm getting an early night tonight ready for New Year's Eve. I'm taking Jake to the Gumbollings', but meeting Alex at five to twelve.

Kim.

P.S. The fancy dress party sounds great. Trust me mam to go as Bo Peep. I suppose Gary came as Larry the Lamb.

Home

CHRISTMAS WEEK

Dear Mam,

Your card arrived today. Nan has had so many she's given yours to the lady in the next door bed. She's dying to get out. She can't survive without her early morning cup of tea.

She has begged them to give her a cup and a kettle and she'll provide her own teabags but sister said that wouldn't help as since the cuts they are not allowed to boil water. I am now taking her in a flask. Yesterday I made her some stew. She won't touch what they have there. She says it's not natural for beef to grow in mountains.

Janice and Damien have asked if they can stay 'til she comes home. Things aren't working out for them in the Tower. Mrs Webster has had to go on to high dosage Librium and the other day Janice found her popping the cat's worming pills. I've said they can stay as long as they pay their way. Then I can save up for a few things before Nan gets back. She'll die of cold if I don't replace the lavatory seat.

Yes thank you, I had some lovely presents (thank Gary for the tape by the way. He *does* sound a bit like Bono/Feargal Sharkey). Ruth gave me a book of poems. Jake said they were simple-mindedly feminist, but I really enjoyed them. I read them while he watched a load of films about blokes killing each other on Boxing Day. Alex enrolled me in Greenpeace and CND and Nan knitted me a jumper and gave me a bobble hat from St Agnes's Christmas Fayre.

Must stop now as Janice and Damien have just arrived and I've got to help them carry in Damien's weight-lifting equipment.

Happy New Year,
Kim.

P.S. I am glad you got so much use out of *your* Christmas present.

Bed

Dear Tracey,

I am knackered from New Year. Brill. Also from being kept up half the night by Janice and Damien. It's wearing Janice out. She looks skinny enough to break in half and has dark blue smudges under her eyes. Ruth gave her a pound of iron tablets for Christmas.

The Gumbollings' do was weird. Irina asked me to wear black which was just as well as I've only got one party frock and that is black synthetic leather with thong bondage laces. It looked a bit peculiar with a white apron over it, which is what Irina gave me as I went through the door. She also handed me a tray of toasted frogs' legs and told me to 'circulate'. I didn't see Jake for the next hour and when I did he was lying on the leopard skin rug with Dulcima Gatsby on top of him. Jake explained that she was demonstrating a movement in Corinthian dance.

Everyone was kail-eyed. Gordon Gumbolling was waving a pint of vodka and shouting that pre-Aids decadence had disappeared from life. The men he was talking to could hardly stand up and one of them kept trumping. Later the same bloke got me cornered in the cloakroom. He asked me if I'd like a bit of pre-Aids decadence and tried to undo my thongs. Fortunately Irina came in with a Musquash and said 'Mervyn, your wife's being sick in the shrubbery'. I found out later it was Gordon's editor.

I think Irina was on drugs. She said she had to do something to liven herself up. She'd spent two days in bed with pheasant-plucking elbow and was so depressed she hadn't even shaved her legs.

She went to pieces completely when she dropped the kumquat mousse. I found her crying into her fourth Kir Royale so I took her to lie down. Her bed was covered with coats and also with an MP and another man kissing. Irina

104

burst into tears and locked herself in the bathroom. She wouldn't come out even though there was a queue of fifteen people. Gordon entertained them with his thesis on ejaculatory drama while he peed into the weeping fig.

I was run off my feet and not by the dancing! Gordon's new CD of the Beatles was on and a few people were propping each other up to it but you could hardly hear it for the noise of screams and breaking glass and the howls of Douarnier Rousseau who'd been shut up in the cellar.

Hang on there's just been a huge crash upstairs. I think Damien has dropped a dumb bell.

Later.

It was not a dumb bell. It was Janice. Damien and she had had a little tiff.

At eleven forty five I went to look for Jake but I couldn't find him anywhere, not even in the attic where a few people had taken a New Year's resolution to give up post-Aids celebacy. I met Gordon going up the stairs. He said was Jake that little wimp who kept spouting about the need for a national morality? If so he'd just left with Dulcima Gatsby.

The funny thing is I wasn't cross at all.

I ran to meet Alex in the pub at the end of the road. He wished me happy new year and hugged me. We walked about for hours with Alex showing me things. Did you know the Imperial War Museum used to be a nut house? Alex says it is very fitting. He knows South London like the back of his hand though his family come from Glasgow. He's sort of the best of North and South.

> I think I am in love.
> Kim.

Dear Jake,

Thanks for your note. I am so glad you have recovered from your 'anxiety related impotence'. I don't think I'd better see you for a while in case I start it up again.

Happy New Year.
Kim.

P.S. I enclose a bit of Gordon's novel that you might find useful.

"The Proustian splendour of the afternoon had faded to a welcome half light. He lay on the bed in a miasma of melancholy. Oh the pain of the post-coital hour! Her bosky tresses so recently spread across his chest, now twisted into snarling snakes. She had raped him of all being. Plundered and pillaged his citadel like the sack of some great treasure. Oh wretched Lamia! Disguised in guileful girl guise. She was as old as mother nature and as relentless. Her lumbering thighs, so fleet in the dance, had opened to many a fool hardy youth. Sucked and left faint with pale anaemic heart. He struggled to move his love-leadened limbs. Was there no end to her deadly woman-desire?"

Etc. Etc. . . .

MONDAY.

Dear Trace,

I have just come back from the Gumbollings'. It has taken two days to clear up from the party. Gordon's still in bed with a hangover. It took ages to get the ~~navel~~ nouvelle cuisine off the carpet but the worst bit was getting the fag ends out of the fish tank without upsetting the piranha.

At last the only thing left to clear up was a TV personality who had passed out on the sofa. Irina kept

shaking her and saying 'Françoise, Françoise, you're missing breakfast telly'.

I had a note from Jake apologizing. It was written on
Dulcima Gatsby's headed paper. I have not heard from
Alex since he dropped me off at my front door at 6 A.M. on
New Year's Day.

I am definitely *not* in love.

K.

TUESDAY.

Dear Jake,

I am not being 'childish' or 'sulking'. You can accept a lift
home from anyone you like. I am returning your copy of
'Lady Chatterley's Lover' which I think you might need.
Personally I couldn't get past page 121.

Please don't write any more notes on that scented paper.
Marvin thinks it's catnip and goes mad ripping it to pieces.

Yours,
Kim.

Ruth's

WEDNESDAY.

Dear Mam,

No she is still in. The consultant hasn't seen her yet (he's
been in Barbados for Christmas) but the houseman, who's
just finishing his YOPS course in open heart surgery, has
told her she needs a rest. She refuses to take the pills they
give her as she's sure she is being used as a guinea pig.
She's made me promise on the bible they won't get a single
organ. I certainly don't think her brain'd be much use to
medical science.

107

We have completely made up our quarrel now as she's dependent on me to smuggle her fags and brown ale *in* and her tranquillizers *out*. They come in handy for Janice who is having bouts of morning sickness. Ruth says it's waking up next to Damien that does it.

Nan and me've had some great chats. She says she's never had time to just lie and think before. She's told me all about meeting grandad at the skating rink and how they were nearly ice dance champs in 1923. It's hard to imagine grandad moving his feet that fast. He could never even lift them for Nan to scrub round his chair.

Nan got very tearful when she was talking about it. She said 'the miserable old bastard was quite lovable in them days'. Then she told me about the happiest time in her life. It was after grandad died. For three years she was courted by a Chelsea pensioner. She said she could've married him but for his false leg. She couldn't abide to see it hanging from the bed post first thing in the morning. She even had a soft spot for Mr Bibby at one time. Harold was a laugh she said, he used to do a wonderful trick with his false teeth. Then she went off into wheezy laughter and wouldn't tell me any more. When she calmed down she wiped her eyes and said yes, she *had* been loved. I suppose you *could* count nicking a person's underwear as a token of affection.

I am going to Sharpe's tomorrow after the New Year Holiday.

Kim.

FRIDAY.

Dear Trace,

Saw Alex at Sharpe's today. I was stacking shelves with South African orange juice when he walked by talking to Stella Shaw. He gave me an off-hand nod and a wave and

then disappeared until tea break. At tea break he had a meeting with the management board so I ate his share of chocolate digestives. At going home time his bike was padlocked to the dustbins as usual but there was no sign of him so I went. Don't know what I saw in him anyway.

I have agreed to meet Jake for a 'one to one session'.

Kim.

3. am

Dear Nan,

sorry I could not make visiting
hour yesterday. I was locked in a cell at
the police station. Jake has just bailed
me out so don't worry. I will definitely
see you tomorrow.

love Kim

MONDAY.

Dear Mam,

Nan should not have rung you up and panicked you. I am fine. I have only got a slight chip on one front tooth. It was all a mistake and the community policeman *has* apologized.

Irina got arrested again for stealing a vibrator (actually she wasn't stealing it, she'd picked it up for a closer look, she'd never seen a black one), Gordon was waiting for a call from the coast, so I had to go and collect her. No sooner had I walked in than I was thrown to the ground and pinned by four policemen. It turned out they'd just been on a refresher course to recognize dangerous maniacs. One of them thought I was a junkie, two thought I was a radical bomber and the fourth thought I was a police-woman in disguise. They gave us both a cup of hot sweet tea and returned Irina's brassiere.

K.

MONDAY.

Dear Trace,

My 'one to one session' took place in the back of a police car. I had to get Jake to come and identify me at the cop shop. I was dead pissed off. Jake was very smug and kept saying it proved I needed a brotherly shoulder. That's a laugh as my shoulders are bigger than his. He looks dead daft in his Dallas designer anorak. He couldn't demonstrate his feelings as there was a police dog sitting between us so I've agreed to meet him sometime at the centre.

Still haven't seen Alex to talk to. He's always rushing around at work but I'm sure he's avoiding me.

?

Kim.

SATURDAY.

Dear Mam,

It was nothing like that! They thought she was going to hang herself with it.

Nan has discharged herself from hospital. She sneaked out in her dressing gown when the night nurse was in the medication cupboard with the ward orderly. Fortunately the milk man was doing his rounds so she got a lift home on his float. She was delivered with the gold top at half past six in the morning. As it happened I was up holding Janice's head over the kitchen sink so we all sat down and had a cup of tea.

The reason Nan left was she'd heard a rumour all patients over eighty were to volunteer for euthanasia. It's because of the 'cuts'. They can't afford to waste a bed on people who won't get better. Also the lady in the next door had come out of surgery with a hysterectomy and a hernia tuck. I said what was wrong with that and Nan said she only went in for a whitlow.

Marvin climbed on Nan's lap and started purring. Nan said it was the first time for a fortnight she hadn't been 'agitato'.

Love,
Kim.

Dear Alex,

I would really like to have a chat sometime

Dear Alex,

I know you are really busy but . . .

Dear Alex,

I would like . . .

Dear Alex,

. . .

Oh *shit!*

Dear Ruth,

I know there are some things you can't tell even your best friend, but if I had anything wrong . . . you know . . . in the 'personal' department, you would let on wouldn't you? I'd tell you.

  I think.

Kim.

Sharpe's

WEDNESDAY.

Dear Tracey,

Alex has broken his silence. He asked me if I would join in a demo for anti-apartheid. I must admit it wasn't exactly a personal chat as forty stackers and till operators were also at the meeting. But he did look *me* straight in the eye when he said it. He wants us to stop Sharpe's selling imported South African goods. He's made lots of placards and we are to parade up and down the car park with them in between our shifts. Girls on the till are to refuse to check out anything with a South African label and he's pasting up pictures of beaten up black kids over the Outspan counter.

  This is what he has been having all the meetings with the management about. I was dead relieved as he was 'in conference' with Stella Shaw so many times I thought he had taken a fancy to her. She has gone absolutely mental. She's taken to smoking three fags at once and yesterday I saw her sneaking round the kiwi fruit re-labelling it 'Zimbabwe'. When she saw me watching she started screaming that I'd no idea how hard it was to be an executive woman. Who was going to pay for her oestrogen implant if she lost her job!

On Saturday Alex has organized a march. Maybe I'll get a chance to talk to him on it.

Kim.

Dear Trace,

I did. He told me the history of South Africa between Westminster Bridge and Lambeth.

There were 150 people on the march. They'd come from all Sharpe's other shops as well. Alex was amazing. He kept running from front to back of the crowd getting them chanting and singing. Ruth came. She wore a T-shirt with 'castrate a rapist, have a ball' on it. So we did. Have a ball I mean. It was cold but the sun was out and we sang and chanted and joked for six miles. My feet were killing me by the time we got to the end of it. But all I got from Alex was half a hot dog and a firm handshake.

Frustrated,
Kim.

Dear Trace,

I have been sacked from Sharpe's! Stella Shaw said they don't need extra staff after Christmas, but I know perfectly well it's because of the demo! She said she was only doing her job. Someone had to pay for her pole cat's mating fee. I told her what to do with her South African salami!

What am I going to do? Now I won't see Alex at all!!!

Desperate Kim.

The Dole Office

TUESDAY.

Dear Mam,

Nan is fine. She got some new pills from her own doctor and was back at aerobics yesterday. Any road I have got plenty of time to look after her as I have been laid off from Sharpe's.

The vicar gave a service to celebrate Nan's return. We prayed for all the rapists, muggers and football hooligans too. After the sermon, when the vicar rambled on about being kind to alcoholics and gays and Nan and Mrs Salmon played noughts and crosses Lady Leonie Bairstowe-Eve came down from the organ in person to shake Nan's hand. Nan was very pleased and proud though later she told me Lady Leonie was no better than she should be and there was more than *one* organ in that church she'd been known to finger.

Someone is at the door . . .

Will finish this later as a man has come to ask me some questions . . .

TUESDAY.

Dear Trace,

I have had a visit from the Special Branch!! They asked me just about everything except me blood group. Nan even had to get me dad's birth certificate out. Bloody Nora! Nan is now convinced I am an IRA bomber. I feel I should warn Alex but I'm afraid I might be followed. Ruth says don't call him as his phone is bound to be bugged. Help!

K.

Friday

Dear Mum,

Market research.
They wanted to know if we kept any dangerous chemicals on the premises. They took away a tin of Vim and Damien's Swedish body rub.

Fancy forgetting to finish the letter! I'm getting as bad as Nan! Last night she put Marvin's dinner in the oven and ours in the cat bowl on the floor. Ha! Ha!

Kim

Princess Diana learning
Amazing Grace on the
bagpipes at Balmoral.

Mrs Kirby

Lakeland

Wordsworth Walk

off London road

Printed in the E.E.C.

116

Dear Trace,

Alex has just been round to see me. The Special Branch had paid him a visit too. We went for a walk in the park so we could talk without Nan putting a glass to the wall.

He said not to worry. It was him they were really after. But his activities were always totally legal so there was nothing they could do. I said it wasn't exactly nothing searching his place for evidence and frightening all his friends. He said we should be grateful we didn't live in South Africa at least we still *had* friends. Then there was a long silence and we just walked. After a while he took my hand and blew on it to warm it up. We got to the quiet bit of the park where the flashers jump out from behind the bushes and he stopped and put his arms round me. I wanted to ask him why he'd been ignoring me after our wonderful New Year's Eve, but I was that choked up I couldn't say a word. He hugged me very tight and I was sure he was going to kiss me, but at the last minute he turned his head away and said it was getting dark.

I don't understand him. I am sure he feels the same as I do.

> Puzzled,
> Kim.

Polly 'Problems'
'Sugar' Magazine
Fleet Street,
WC1.

Dear Polly,

I am eighteen (nearly), with a 'neat' figure, nice smile and friendly personality. But for some reason, none of the blokes I go out with want to go to bed with me. Well that is . . . at first they *do* then when *I* do they *don't*. I have asked my friends about personal hygiene, but they say apart from a few blackheads I am fine.

I am very worried about this, particularly as my mother (39½) has just got a new boyfriend (18) and they are going at it like knives. Obviously her sexual attraction does not run in the family. Please send any advice under plain cover as my Nanna is dead nosey.

Worried,
Kim.

WEDNESDAY.

Dear Mam,

I am not managing too badly. Of course I've had to sign on again. Irina gives me the odd fiver when she remembers but she is in such a state these days I hardly like to ask. Janice and Damien don't pay rent very often. Nan is dead fed up with them. She has had to replace the jar of marmalade twice this week as they use it to throw at each other. I think it's another 'special' relationship like you had with dad.

It is very cold here too. We have been threatened with snow but none has fallen yet. I bet the hills look beautiful. Do you remember that toboggan ride when we ended up in the farm? Dad took a picture of us covered in Mr Hogbin's pig feed.

Lots of love,
Kim.

P.S. Have just been for the paper and it is starting to snow. Marvin is chasing the flakes in the yard.

Dear Trace,

There is thick snow everywhere. Nan says she has never seen the like in Lambeth and Marvin hasn't stirred from the airing cupboard for days. Last night I put on three layers and two skateboards and skied down to the centre to meet Jake for our session. When I got there, he'd phoned in a message that the buses weren't running up his way and he didn't want to freeze to death by walking. Gordon Gumbolling is right. He *is* a wimp. I tried to ring him up to tell him but my fingers were so cold I couldn't turn the dial. The centre's boiler has broken down and they've been waiting a week for the gas board. It's a good job I was there though as it took quite a few people to dig the inspector out of the boiler room snow drift when he *did* arrive.

No word from Alex.

Kim.

Dear Mam,

I have forbidden Nan to go out to feed the birds as the lady next door but one was found frozen to the washing line with a peg in one hand and her husband's socks in the other. Sorry you are having trouble with the pipes, our kitchen sink is completely frozen too. Unfortunately Janice had been sick in it before she realized so now the kitchen is out of bounds. I phoned the 24-HOUR NEVER LET YOU DOWN INSTANT EMERGENCY PLUMBER, but he was in bed with the 'flu.

Thanks for the Christmas photos. They're very good. Especially the one of Gary sitting on your lap. Dusty looks

119

very thin. Don't let her go out in the snow unless she is wearing my Brownie jumper. You know what her chest is like.

Love,
Kim.

Dear Trace,

Sorry the writing is wobbly. I have got my gloves on. Nan and I are huddled over the electric fire as it's the only warm place in the house. Marvin is sitting right in front of it. He's set fire to his tail twice. We're even sleeping in this room as Nan can't afford to heat the others. Last night Janice joined us as Damien had shoved her out of bed. She said he did it in his sleep but I am not so sure, they'd had words over whose turn it was to wear the nightie.

She is seven months pregnant now and looks like a stick insect carrying a football. She's not very well though. She says the baby is a kicker like his father. Must stop as Nan wants me to help her fill in a form to win a holiday in the sun.

Brrr
K.

FRIDAY.

Dear Mam,

Have got a job clearing snow for the council. It's a very mixed bunch of people. The oldest is 93. He says it's warmer shovelling four foot of snow than sitting in his flat. The council pay £15 a day which is £10 more than the heating allowance. A bag of coal and a box of wood costs £6 in London!

120

Today I found out it was a one day job. The thaw has set in.

Irina has just dropped a note through asking if I'll babysit Gordon tonight while she goes to her 'channelling' session. He's working on a piece on the male menopause and gets very depressed if there's no-one's shoulder to cry on. She will give me an extra fiver as it's heavy work. I don't mind leaving Nan as she and Janice are quite happy winding wool and talking about the baby. Damien hasn't been seen for days.

Kim.

Dear Alex,

I desperately need your 'advice'. Something has happened to 'a friend' and I don't know what to do. Remember what we talked about in the park? Well it is a bit like that. Can we meet 'you know where', 'you know when'. It is *urgent!*'

K.

Dear Tracey,

Shock horror! Clovis has been arrested. Ruth and me were walking up her street last night after rock climbing at the Recreation Centre, when a police car nearly ran us down as it swerved around the corner. They were doing 90 with their lights flashing and sirens going. As Ruth's road is a cul de sac they had to pull up rather sharp. Ruth thought her mam must have been taken ill (the day before she'd been dragged along the road by her handbag when the bus driver shut it in the exit for a joke). We ran into the house and straight away there were bullets whizzing all round us.

It was like watching 'Cagney and Lacey' except they were aiming at us. The room was crammed with policemen and three were throttling Clovis. As one of them said afterwards, they weren't to know he had asthma.

Fortunately the bullets were rubber so they only dented the furniture and gave Selvin a nasty ear ache, but in the end three stretchers had to be brought in. One for Clovis, who'd gone a pale blue colour, one for Ruth who was knocked unconscious when a chair broke on her head and one for Mrs Baptiste who fainted when she came in from bible class and found her Capo Di Monte shattered.

I went down to the station with them. The second time this month! They took my fingerprints and charged Clovis with breaking and entering and resisting arrest. I was there for hours before they decided I was not one of the gang.

On my way home I went via Alex. There were no lights on so I dropped a note through his letter box. I hope he understands it! He's the only person who'll know what to do.

Yours in terror,
Kim.

TUESDAY.

Dear Trace,

Met Alex in Sharpe's car park when he finished work. He was great. We went straight to the Law Centre to talk to his friend the community lawyer. He rang the police station and they said Clovis had just come round and they were going to court in the morning.

This morning me and Ruth and Alex and Lloyd (the lawyer) went to the magistrate's court. Clovis was charged with seventeen offences including the robbery at Nan's! Lloyd made an application for bail but the police said

122

Clovis was a danger. The magistrate said he found that hard to believe as Clovis is only five foot tall and was wearing a sling and a neck brace. But the police insisted he was violent and had tried to strangle himself in the van. He's been remanded in custody until the trial.

We were allowed to see him for a few minutes before he was taken back to the cells. Lloyd told him they would get a Crown Court trial as his only hope was a jury. Ruth and me were crying and after a while so was Clovis.

Alex had to rush off to work but he said he would call round to see how I was this evening. Can't wait! It's Nan's Cordon Bleu night at the centre and I have told Janice to stay out 'til late. Damien has still not returned.

12.30

Alex has just gone. He told me to cheer up, Lloyd got a first at Law School. I don't know what else we talked about. All I know is that whenever he looks at me a funny feeling starts in my knees and goes right the way up to my tummy. I am definitely in love.

Kim.

Dear Scotch,

How long did Cheyenne get for kicking that policeman in the ~~balls~~ ~~cobblers~~ ~~nuts~~ crutch? Hope you are well and had a nice time on your holidays.

All the best,
Kim.

FRIDAY.

Dear Trace,

Clovis's trial is in two weeks' time. It's the same day as my birthday. To think I've been here nearly a year! I found a photo of you and me on Morcambe pier the other day. You wouldn't recognize me now. My hair and clothes are completely different. It's funny because I don't remember changing. Alex is taking me to a concert on the South Bank tonight. It's in aid of Nicaragua.

Kim.

SATURDAY.

Dear Trace,

Alex kissed me.

We were walking along the South Bank under the railway arch and he was explaining about third world poverty. He stopped to give some money to a busker and I bent down to tie my bootlace and when I stood up we sort of bumped into each other. The next thing we were kissing wildly and he had me up against the side of the tunnel. The busker was so amazed he pushed the wrong button on his rhythm machine and Alex and me were necking to a military march. When we'd finished we both leant against the wall shaking. Though that could have been because a train was going overhead.

Alex looked in shock. He still didn't say anything though. Aren't men weird?

Kim.

Lesley Hewitt MP,
House of Commons,
Westminster.

Dear Sir/Madam,

A friend of mine has been arrested for some things he definitely did not do. I know because he was with me and his sister at a rapping contest when he was supposed to have been breaking into a video shop. Various people swore they saw him but one described him as six foot four inches, one as about forty and one as grey-haired with a limp. He is small, 17 and did not limp before he went to the police station. Will you see what you can do?

Also, can you get rid of Cruise missiles, put up pensions, run more buses, ban nuclear power, save the whale and castrate rapists?

Yours sincerely,
Kim Kirby.

The Infirmary

WEDNESDAY.

Dear Trace,

Janice is in premature labour. Damien came back this morning with a van and started to load his nautilus. It was his way of saying he was moving out. Of course Janice tried to stop him and she ended up in the rockery with the pocket off his running shorts. Nan came out and found her rolling around clutching herself and groaning so we went next door to phone for an ambulance straight away. It didn't come straight away as the hospital couldn't find one. Eventually as it looked as though she couldn't wait the community policeman took her down on his crossbar. Ruth and me have been here three hours. Ruth is pacing up and down as though *she* is the expectant father.

Later.

A nurse has just come and told us Janice has had the baby. We're going to see it in the incubator.

Later.

It's got all its arms and legs and things and a scrunched up face like a squirrel. Ruth said it would have been better if it *had* been a squirrel. Trust the stupid cow to give birth to another *boy*.

K.

Dear Mam,

Is it really that long since I've written? It must be because nothing much has happened.

Janice has had her baby, she is calling it Damien II. Damien I has gone to live with his gym instructor. I am not going out with Jake any more. He has decided he needs a mother figure. I suppose that's how Gary feels about you?

Yes some money would be nice for my birthday. Then I could buy some new spring clothes. All my trousers are worn out. Nan says she doesn't know how I can tell the difference, they all had holes in to start with.

She is back to normal. Yesterday she threw a strawberry yoghurt at a woman from Help the Aged. It was very unfair, the lady was only trying to give out food surplus to help the poor and needy.

The snow has completely gone and there are some crocuses out in the rockery.

Love,
Kim

The day before my birthday

Dear Tracey,

Thanks for the card. It arrived this morning but I opened it as tomorrow I'll be too nervous. I am a witness for the defence! Lloyd says I have got to make a good impression so I have borrowed Nan's 'Function' suit and fox furs. Now I look as though I am going to launch a ship. I've got my

126

St Agnes bobble hat to cover my hair — now silver with yellow tips — and a pair of string gloves in case my hands start to sweat. Must stop as Marvin has got the fox fur by the tail and is throwing it about and growling. Nan says he's only being friendly. He probably thinks they are related.

Yours nervously,
Kim.

6.30 A.M. but really still my birthday

Dear Tracey,

God. I have never had a birthday like this one before!

The trial went on all day. Me and Ruth had to stay in a special room until we'd given evidence. Mrs Baptiste was still in intensive care but Irina Gumbolling sat in the public gallery to be supportive. Clovis looked very small. He could hardly see over the dock. The judge kept asking him to speak up until the clerk of the court went and turned his hearing aid on.

The chief superintendent said his voices had led him to Clovis. He had been driving home from his Masonic Lodge when suddenly a bollard had crashed into the car. He'd seen stars and then Clovis Baptiste written in the sky. The judge asked him how many he'd had to drink. Lloyd then explained that Clovis's name was graffiti sprayed up on the railway bridge. He and his mates had done it to celebrate getting the dole. Next I was called and asked about the bread knife. They had found Clovis's fingerprints on it. I explained that Clovis and Ruth had been to tea the day before and Clovis had made us all bread and jam sandwiches. Then there was the evidence of a video in his room. At first Clovis wasn't very keen to talk about it, but when Lloyd pressed him he said he'd bought it from a DC for fifty quid in the pub.

The jury was out for ages.

Irina took me and Ruth to a wine bar while we waited. She said after all it was my birthday. Ruth and I had a coffee and she had a double vodka. She said she'd had a channelling session the previous night and her spirit guide had promised her the damages would be slight. Ruth said he must have meant the injuries as Selvin was deaf in one ear.

There was a terrible hush in the court. All you could hear was the whistling of the judge's hearing aid. Then the jury filed back in and I searched their faces for signs of kindness. They looked like 'The Twelve Angry Men' except that two of them were women. The foreman stood up and we all shut our eyes tight until we heard 'Not Guilty'! Lloyd led the cheering, which was loud enough to drown out the prosecution's mutters though I did catch one calling Lloyd a black bastard. The judge told Clovis he could go but fined him £10 for the graffiti. Irina said her spirit guide was right as usual then she paid the fine and drove us all home in Gordon's Volvo.

Nan had got Guinness and a chocolate cake for tea so we all went back to our house for a celebration and after a bit Alex arrived with a bottle of Sharpe's champagne and we drank Black Velvets to Clovis's release and my birthday. Alex stood on a chair to propose the toast and when he said 'And here's to Kim, may she get the key to her door . . .' his eyes met mine and a tremble went right through me.

We all got smashed. Nan had to be put to bed after her fourth go at 'Knees up Mother Brown'. She was going to sing the fifth one *on* the table. Irina left to pick up Gordon who cannot travel on buses and Ruth and Clovis went to visit Mrs Baptiste.

There was just me and Alex left.

I don't know how to describe what happened next.

I have come of age.

Kim.

The day after my birthday

Dear Mam,

Thanks for the birthday card. It's only a day late but I hope you remember that I am eighteen and not eight which is the number on it.

Yes I had a great time thanks. It's amazing how much older you can get in one day.

Nan and I went to the pub at lunchtime today. It was the first time I have not had to stand outside with a ginger ale and a packet of crisps. I still had to stop Nan offering the bus conductor half fare for me though.

Janice has been allowed to take Damien II home. He has grown little tufts of ginger hair and is either sleeping or waving his fists. Janice says he is the dead spit of his father. By the way what made you think Damien I was 'of the other persuasion'? His gym instructor is called Sonia and is the South-East body building champion. Janice says she does not care if she never sees him again. She and Mrs Webster are starting a women's group in the Tower.

Love,
Kim.

P.S. You did not sign the card 'from Gary'. Is he still living in my bedroom?

WEDNESDAY.

Dear Tracey,

I *would* give you details but it's embarrassing to write about. Anyway there is nothing to say it will be like that for you and Nigel, even if you have bought some lime-flavoured condoms. One thing though, I am glad I never did it with Jake. Irina says he's doing a lot of primal screaming. Dulcima's next-door neighbour told her. I saw him out with Dulcima in the park the other day. She was pushing him in her shopping trolley and he was sucking his thumb.

With Alex it is the *real thing*.

I must admit it hurt a bit at first but that was mostly trying to get the cap in. The first time it shot out and gave Marvin an awful surprise. But Alex was very gentle and knew exactly what to do. After all he is twenty-five. We lay in front of the gas fire with Nan's knitting bag for a pillow. It was like being in two places at once. Sort of watching from the ceiling as well as being on the floor. Now I know what Irina is going on about! We made quite a lot of noise but what with Marvin purring and Nan snoring I don't think anyone noticed – it was what Nan would call a Family Occasion.

About six o'clock it was getting light so Alex got up and

made us a cup of tea. I was dying to tell him all the things I was feeling but instead we just sat hand in hand drinking our tea until we heard Nan putting a foot out of bed and groping about for the chamber pot. At the door he kissed me again and held me very tight. I just had time to grab my T-shirt before Nan came tottering down the stairs.

I haven't seen him since but yesterday a dozen red roses arrived. It must be because he's older that he's so romantic.

Love, Love, Love,
Kim.

THURSDAY.

Dear Mam,

I didn't realize the whole band was now living in my bedroom. No wonder the neighbours are complaining. Mr Wigley always used to make a fuss if I drew my curtains too loudly.

It is very awkward having paying guests. Especially if they don't pay you. As I found out with Janice and Damien.

You'll have to be firm and ask them to go. Nan says people always take advantage of a woman on her own.

Love,
Kim.

South-West 'Special' Clinic

MONDAY.

Dear Tracey,

No, I do not think it is a good idea for you and Nigel to have a 'try out'.

I have not seen Alex for a week. I am desperate. I am

now sure I am pregnant/have got Aids. I know that's ridiculous, there was enough rubber between us to make a pair of Wellingtons but still . . .

Wait.

Kim.

Dear Tracey,

What a shame my letter came a day too late. I must say I would have chosen a more private place than the old cricket pavilion, I'm not surprised the earth did not move for you. Actually you were lucky it didn't cave in completely, those floor boards haven't been replaced for years.

My mother is having a difficult time with Gary. She says she only sees him when he comes down to the kitchen to make coffee and raid the fridge. His band are working on a new demo tape. They've been signed by 'Rooster Records'.

No He has not been round. I happened to walk up his street several times last night, but there were no lights on.

Kim.

SATURDAY.

Dear Mam,

Of course you were right to get cross. It's one thing having a deep freeze full of rats but quite another finding a live python in the bathroom.

Do you think he has gone for good?

Kim.

132

Dear Alex,

Thank you for your postcard. Of course I will meet you for a talk when you get back.

Kim x

P.S. What exactly are you doing in Buddleigh Salterton?

Princess Diana watching
Prince Charles toss a caber.

Alex Blythe
Crumbe Cottage

B

133

Maire Trayner,
c/o The Daily Stab.
Fleet Street,
WC1

Dear Maire,

Just recently I let a boyfriend ~~fuck make love to~~ 'go all the way'. Now to my horror I have discovered he is a married man! He says he tried to resist the temptation and begs me to forgive him. What should I do?

Confused,
Kim (18)

P.S. He and his wife are having a trial separation.

P.P.S. I fancy him rotten.

THURSDAY.

Dear Tracey,

Thanks for the packet of 'Tickle your Fancy' rubbers, the one with the shredded wheat coating certainly looks fun. I don't think I shall have much use for them though as Alex and I are not going out any more.

He has just been to Devon to see his wife.

When he came back he took me out for a meal and said he'd never meant what we did on my birthday to happen but no-one should be alone on their eighteenth birthday. He made it sound like he was doing me a favour. I was that mad I tore the fake carnation on our bistro table to pieces.

He said I mustn't misunderstand. He really cared for me but he didn't want to involve me in a messy situation. I said in that case we shouldn't be eating spaghetti bolognese. It is hard enough to keep it on your fork when you are not emotionally distraught.

134

He walked me home and by the time we got to Nan's front door we were both in tears. Me because I couldn't bear the thought that I would not see him again and him because he had drunk a bottle and a half of red wine. Marvin was in the yard calling next door but one's tabby. I was dead jealous.

Kim.

P.S. Are you absolutely certain Nigel hasn't got a 'past'.

SATURDAY.

Dear Mam,

I am sorry you are so low. You are quite right, all men are ~~rassskats~~ pigs. You couldn't have expected it to last for ever with Gary though, he was bound to find someone more his own type. I must say the lead singer of the 'Butch Bike Girls' is an odd choice though.

I *will* think about coming home for a bit. As it happens I am quite ~~pissed off~~ fed up with London. It is difficult at the moment as I am typing out Gordon's novel (I am faster with two fingers than he is with ten) and I don't want my last source of money to come to an end. Irina has been much better since she started channelling. She has persuaded Dulcima Gatsby to join. Jake has moved in with Dulcima. She's got an attic where he can put his train set out.

Nan sends her best.

Love,
Kimmie x

Dear Tracey,

It's a bit sudden isn't it? I know you have had your trousseau ready for years but two weeks . . .! Being married doesn't make you 'sure' of anyone as you put it. Alex's wife was not 'sure' of him was she?

Saw him in Sharpe's the other day when I called to get Nan's All Bran. He was collecting signatures for a petition to outlaw nuclear dumping. He is more in love with politics than he'll ever be with a woman. He grinned and waved as though nothing had happened. I was that mad I went and spread my reply from Maire Trayner on his clipboard. It was a life-size picture of a willy with instructions on how to roll a condom on.

K.

THURSDAY.

Dear Mam,

My last source of money *has* come to an end. Irina Gumbolling has eloped with Dulcima Gatsby. They fell in love at a channelling session. They had a mystical experience when Dulcima 'became' the spirit of a Greek poetess and danced an Iambic Pentameter with no clothes on.

Also they had both gone right off men. Irina said she could no longer stand Gordon's awful habits (he is mad about American TV series) and Dulcima said Jake was the last straw. She put up with the bottle-feeding every four hours but when he started wanting his nappies changed she just couldn't take any more.

They have gone to Llangollen to 'find bliss'. I am not sure they will find it in Llangollen. I went there on a school trip once and everything was closed.

I haven't got a bean. Tracey is getting married in a fortnight. I have been here a year and if it wasn't for the emergency fund Nan keeps in the back of the piano I wouldn't even be able to buy her a present. Why am I so unemployable? I really try and I'm not thick. I'm nearly always polite and I work hard when I get a chance. But nobody will give it me.

Kim.

H.R.H. Haddock,
Finney Place,
Lambeth.

Dear Mr Haddock,

I'm applying for the job of Trainee Fishmonger, which appeared in last month's Angling Times.

Personally I am not that fond of fish. I always feel sorry for them, staring up at you with their little eyes. When my dad used to take me fishing I always threw them back. My cat Marvin is mad for a fish head though. So if we have any left overs at the end of the day, I can always dispose of them for you.

I'm sure we will get on swimmingly,

Yours,
Kim Kirby.

SATURDAY.

Dear Mam,

I cried all night when I got your letter. I cannot believe that Dusty is no more. What was an articulated lorry doing in our road anyway? It is hardly wide enough for Mr Wigley's wheelchair. It's all my fault for adopting Marvin.

I wouldn't speak to him all day and wouldn't let him in the bed when I was clutching Dusty's photo. He didn't understand at all as he usually licks my tears. Dusty must be buried with full honours. You are not to give her to the dustman. She must be put in the nettle patch dad used to call 'my' garden and then in the Summer butterflies will dance over her head.

Must stop. Marvin is sitting outside the door scratching the carpet and me-owing to be let in.

Kimmie.

MONDAY.

Dear Mam,

Scotch Salmon has just been round to see us. He wants Nan to sponsor him to slim for charity. He is a reformed character since Cheyenne blew himself up.

He has pledged to lose ten stone for a cot death unit at the local hospital. He got quite tearful telling us all about the poor little babies who were smothered in their sleep. Nan was furious. She said it was the third charity who'd been round that week *and* she's saving milk bottle tops towards the community bus. I thought about Janice's baby and its tiny little fists so I said I would support Scotch. Nan said she hoped I wasn't going to do it single-handed, it would take a crane to lift him.

Scotch was dead grateful. He pressed ten quid into my hand as he left and said he knew it didn't cover what he owed me but the VAT had taken all the rest. If only I had another £20 I could be home for Dusty's funeral.

Love,
Kim.

Dear Mam,

He was sniffing lighter fluid and his girlfriend lit a match. Cheyenne lost his eyebrows and the Cortina he was sitting in. The police tried to do her for attempted manslaughter but she said it was Cheyenne's own fault, he knew she was a chain smoker and he'd already emptied her lighter.

It was a big shock for Scotch and Tara especially as they had just sold up the business in time to stop Scotch going to prison. They have both become Christians and Tara is organizing Latin American Nights at the town hall to pay for keeping Cheyenne's paraplegic ward.

Love,
Kim.

P.S. Cheyenne can still kick a football around as he's got the use of one leg.

P.P.S. The postman has just been. He left a postcard from Irina. It has a picture of a waterfall and says 'Torrents released I have never known before'. I suppose it *does* rain a lot in Wales. Or she could have been referring to the amount Gordon cried when she left him. He has completely gone to pieces and I've had to do everything for him. He didn't even know where the frying pan was kept. I caught him trying to grill bacon in front of Irina's sun lamp.

Later.

I have just got back from Gordon's. I had to wash and iron 38 shirts. That was not so bad but searching the house for them first was exhausting! Why *does* a bloke take his shirt off in the cellar? Three of his best were in Douarnier Rousseau's basket.

While I was ironing Gordon came in to the kitchen to make himself a cup of coffee. But he couldn't find it. Or the kettle. While I made it for him, he read me out chunks of his novel, which depressed him so much he started to cry again. He has finished it now and the publisher says it is 'tough, convincing and muscular', which is more than you can say for Gordon.

He has given me a list of instructions for getting him to New York. He's taking a sabbatical to research a short book on great American thinkers. He always said he had one foot in the Atlantic. Irina said he was referring to the time he went paddling in the Hebrides. His list begins 'Note books, pens and valium for the journey . . .' and he has enclosed a cheque for his airfare and £20 wages for me. He has no idea how to deal with Travel Agents. Irina always did it for him. I will go there in the morning and get his ticket and mine.

See you tomorrow,
Kim.

DUSTY
Dusty queen of all the cats
Though not fond of chasing rats
A chicken breast for you to eat
Will be at the Pearly Gates to greet
And endless time for you to rest
On chairs and cushions of the best
Without harsh voice calling you a louse
for bringing fleas into the house
Or sitting on my Mam's best hat
Or peeing on the bathroom mat.
love
Kim

'Lakeland',
Wordsworth Walk,
Off London Road.

SATURDAY.

Dear Nan,

Mam had to bury Dusty before I got there. It had turned
quite mild and she said she wouldn't keep. I have planted
a violet on her grave. I would have liked a bigger show but
Mam says it will spread like nobody's business as it is only
a weed.

Gary has written a song to commemorate her. Mam says
he always preferred the cat to her but that was probably
because Dusty used to bring him headless mice as presents.
The Song.

> Oh Dusty
> Yeah
> Oh Dusty
> Yeah
> Oh Dusty
> Yeah Yeah Yeah
> Oh Dusty

There's a lot more but you can't really hear it as he goes
mad with a guitar solo and ends by bashing his amplifier
to bits.

Give Marvin a kiss for me. I am glad you've got him for
company but I do miss him (and you of course).

Tracey and Nigel are getting married on Saturday. They
are having a fork and finger at Heatherview Hall where
they have got peacocks and a fountain in the grounds. A JP
was found dancing naked in it after the Masons' Christmas
party. Tracey has invited me as long as I borrow anything
from her wardrobe. She is doing her own and all the
bridesmaids' hair and has offered to give me a soft curl

perm. Mam sends her best and thanks you for having me, especially as it was for a year. She is giving me driving lessons as a belated birthday present.

Love,
Kim.

P.S. What did the social worker who came to visit you want?

Complaints Department,
British Rail.

Dear Madam/Sir,

I recently made a long journey. Also a starving one. The buffet was closed due to 'failure of equipment'. The Guard was nearly crying when he announced the boiler had burst.

I paid £30 for my ticket which is all the money I get for a week. My seat was covered with tea and full of another person for the first fifty miles. The Guard very kindly let me sit on a crate of chickens in his van and we had quite a chat while he was clipping my ticket. He said he was taking early retirement as he couldn't stand the strain. Three guards had thrown themselves off the trains due to customer aggravation. The buffet manager had been on valium since a traveller had forced him to drink his own coffee and he himself had had a BR sandwich shoved up his nose.

He does not enjoy being hated and I do not enjoy sitting for three hundred miles with wet trousers and a rumbling stomach. Can you do something about it please?

Yours faithfully,
Kim Kirby.

P.S. The rest of the journey was very nice. All the little lambs were out and the fields were green and sunny.

Dear Ruth,

Thanks a lot for walking Nan to Bingo. She really likes you now and says how polite and helpful you are. Don't you think joining the police force is going a bit far though?

Nothing has changed up here, except Tracey. She wears pearly pink nail varnish and high-heeled shoes. She says she has to keep herself smart for the salon. She and Nigel are getting a new 'cottage style' bungalow out on the London road. Nigel is giving her unit trusts for her wedding present. He's trying to get promotion at the bank.

There is still no work. I answered an advert for 'attractive barmaid', the manageress didn't think I qualified, and I did have a one day job in a funeral parlour. It would have been longer, but I fainted when I saw the bits of a road crash victim being put back together.

As for social life. Forget it. I went to the local for a lager and blackcurrant. There was a rock band playing 'Route 66'. They were all at least forty and wearing bell-bottomed denims.

It's Tracey's wedding tomorrow. Maybe I'll meet somebody there.

I am glad you made it up with Janice. Her women's group sounds fab. Whose idea was the mock castrating? Bet Mr Webster was scared.

Wish I was coming to Greenham with you.

All the best,
Kim.

Dear Nan,

What does she mean 'sheltered acccommodation'? What's wrong with the accommodation you've got? It's got a roof.

Great news about the community bus. Scotch really has turned over a new leaf! Of course when he says 'it needs work' he probably means it hasn't got an engine but still . . . Did he manage to salvage any other stock when he had to sell the yard? You'll have to get someone to look after it and take you on your trips. What a pity the vicar lost his driving licence.

Tracey's wedding was everything you'd expect. You would have loved it. I borrowed Mam's Top Shop executive woman's suit. (Did I tell you she's got a job in an Estate Agent's now?) It looked a bit weird with a growing out Mohican but everybody was too drunk to notice.

Nigel's friends all play rugby so they made a team of honour at the entrance of the church and Tracey was thrown from hand to hand like a rugby ball when she got out of the limo. The captain threw her over his shoulder and ran up the aisle to make a try. Her bridesmaids had an awful job trying to keep up.

Heatherview Hall is very nice. The grounds were out of bounds owing to a nuclear accident at the power station next door. They said there was no danger to the public but a waitress told me the goldfish in the pond were floating belly up that morning. We had lobster soup, terrine of trout, sole mornay and jumbo shrimp. I only hope it wasn't local.

The wine was 'Methode Champenoise' which means it gives you an awful hangover. Nigel started his before the disco was over. He was found slumped under the table with the Roughmere Rambler's full back.

They have gone to Jersey for their honeymoon to see the lovely spring flowers.

Lots of love,
Kim.

Dear Ruth,

I have been on a CND demo. I was on my way to Tracey's reception at the time and the car I was in was stopped and covered with posters and several people sat on the bonnet wearing world war two gas masks. They were protesting at a leak of poison gas at a nuclear plant nearby. The driver of the hire car was furious. He said they were all in the pay of the Russians and ought to be put down. He wouldn't get out of the car without a muffler round his face though in case what they said was true.

I didn't mind. I reckon I breathed enough carbon monoxide in London to make me immune to owt else. I walked along with them and sang 'The Spirit, she is like a Mountain' until a fifteen stone WPC stopped us. Tracey was furious. She said I'd ruined her wedding and what did I think I was doing bringing these daft ideas up North.

I don't feel I fit in here any more.

Kim.

CND Coffee Shop

WEDNESDAY.

Dear Janice,

I enclose some song sheets that I have got from the local branch of the CND for songs to sing on demos. I agree that Rod Stewart's Greatest Hits are not quite right, but you have got to start somewhere and I am sure your mother meant well.

I am glad she is so much better. I am sure banning Errol and your father from the flat has something to do with it.

How far through the fence had she got when she was arrested? I have never heard of anyone cutting it with their teeth before. The picture of you and Damien II stuck to the fence with disposable nappies was a very good likeness. It was printed in 'The Guardian' but I did not see it until yesterday as I have to order it specially up here and it is always a few days late.

What exactly did Ruth say to the police to stop them arresting you? It cannot have been her usual language!

Please keep in touch. I've got no-one to talk to here.

Kim.

Peak Side Shopping Centre

SATURDAY.

Dear Nan,

Tell the bloody busybody to piss off. They cannot make you move if you don't want to.

Mam is thinking of moving. Working in an estate agent's is a great temptation. She says this house has too many memories. I saw her turning over a photograph album the other day and crying. Later I had a look and it was full of pictures of her and dad at the sea side. It's funny to think they were once young and in love. I asked her if she was upset at remembering the good times they had together and she said no, they always had their worst rows on holiday.

She's really enjoying this new job though and is a completely different person. I hope you won't mind me saying that she has been out once or twice with her boss Marcus Beavor, of Beavor, Hunt and Fortune, and it is nice to see her looking pretty . . . well . . . *alive* again.

My driving lessons are going well. I cannot wait to get

them over. Once you know how an engine works the rest is obvious.

Have those daffs I planted come up? Don't let Marvin pee on them.

You do not mention him pining but I'm sure he is.

Love,
Kim.

Watch out girls!

Dear Ruth,

Can you go round and look at me Nan. She is getting herself in a right state because Social Services want to put her in special accommodation. They say she is too poorly to be left on her own. But their home for OAPs is on a one in two hill and I can't see how that could be good for her angina.

I don't know how to take the news that you are going to the Police Recruitment Centre. You said the visit to Greenham Common left a lasting impression but I thought you meant the black eye. I understand that you want to give a public service and I suppose you might as well get paid for beating people up . . . but what makes you think they are only human too?

Worried,
Kim.

Dear Nan,

They said *what*! Just let them try to force you out. Get Ruth to talk to the social worker and explain that you're not on your own, you've got *Marvin*.

I've put in for my driving test. Marcus says I ought to pass it. He's been giving me some extra lessons in his BMW. Me and Mam and him drove to the sea on Sunday. It was nice and sunny but we didn't pick any mussels as the beach is well polluted. We got back in half the time as I drove. Marcus said I did very well and Mam went to bed with a migraine.

Kim

Dear Ruth,

You can't go joining the police because a WPC lent you a hanky to stop your nose bleed. Especially as she had given it to you in the first place. Bloody Nora! I suppose she also told you it was half past time to go and helped you cross the road to a Black Maria!

As Nan says one swallow doth not a birdbath make . . . or something . . . and nor doth one WPC. A police force make I mean. Or an arrest either. She won't get promotion for giving you a fag and a cup of tea and telling you she too believes in the aims of the Greenham protestors. She can't

148

believe in them that much if she knicked your balloons and your sparklers.

What about your friends! At this rate you will end up arresting Janice and her Mam. You know how violent things can get when you go on those Peace marches!

Your ex-friend Kim.

MONDAY.

Dear Nan,

Marvin is going to the Battersea Dogs Home over my dead body! Yours too if it brings on your angina. It is all very well for the social worker to say you can only stay if you have a member of your family. Some people haven't got a member. Can't the vicar take her up about it? St Agnes's would not be the same without you. Who would give Jesus a polish on every alternate Friday?

Don't give in,
Kim.

The Reverend St John Toper,
St Agnes The Martyr,
Church Street,
Clapham.

Dear Reverend Toper,

I do appreciate your concern for my grandmother. She told me how you accosted the social worker in 'The Jolly Cockney' (whilst delivering the parish magazine), she must have been surprised to hear a vicar say 'Bog Off!'

Nan is old and frail of course but she has plenty of fighting spirit as the social worker found out when she tried to take Marvin away. Apparently her ear lobe has been

149

sewn back on (Marvin hates to be picked up by strangers) but she still has concussion from the blow with the rolling pin.

Nan mentioned you were looking for a mechanic to fix the community bus? Are there any wages?

The blessings of God be upon you,

Kim.

FRIDAY.

Dear Ruth,

I am so glad you've abandoned the idea of joining the police because

A) The recruiting officer referred to you as a 'Nig Nog'.

B) WPCs do not get issued with truncheons. You are expected to hit dangerous criminals with your handbag.

C) Clovis said he would never speak to you again.

How are you going to give a public service now?

Your re-friend,
Kim.

MONDAY.

Dear Mrs Salmon,

Thank you so much for writing to tell me about being rescued by my friend Ruth. She certainly *is* very strong . . . though I don't know about 'especially for a girl', after all she has been carrying her little brothers and all the shopping around for years. Still, bending iron railings back with your bare hands isn't easy. How did your head get between them in the first place? It's a good job your garden is on her way home from the bus stop!

150

Hope you haven't suffered any other ill effects and the collar isn't keeping you from going to Social Sequence.

Best wishes,
Kim.

'The Fighting Cock'

WEDNESDAY.

Dear Nan,

I passed my driving test today! I was that nervous sweat was blinding me and my hands were stuck to the steering wheel before we'd gone a yard. I had to do two emergency stops. One when the examiner asked me to and one when an old man in a Mercedes overshot a red light. The examiner said he thought it was the mayor.

Marcus and Mam are taking me to 'The Peking Duck' for a treat.

Fab and Brillo!
Kim.

SATURDAY.

Dear Ruth,

I had a crashing headache this morning (do not touch Shanghai Slings in a Chinese cocktail bar) so it was a bit of a shock when I opened your letter and a fireman fell out! I had to have four Alka Seltzers before I recognized you. Especially as the helmet comes right down to your nose. It was nice of Mrs Salmon to give you a reference. Fancy her getting stuck in her garden railings trying to scoop 10p off the pavement with her trowel. Still, 'It's an ill wind' as Nan would say. Actually she doesn't say 'ill wind'.

151

She is still in trouble with the Social Services. They have marked her file 'abusively aggressive'. She had a snitch when the new social worker was searching for the bathroom. She was outraged! She says she only called him a dickhead when he asked if she *preferred* no running hot water. I hope she does not get smart when he asks her a simple question like say 'where do you want this pint of milk putting', or he could have her sectioned! They've already got Mrs Salmon to say she can't add up at Pontoon.

If *only* I could get a job I'd come back like a shot. I like the hills and trees and that, but everything is so *green*!

Kim.

P.S. Thanks for enclosing a fire-fighter application form but I don't think I'd qualify as I'm not at least 5′6″.

The Reference Library

MONDAY.

Dear Nan,

Elizabeth is the Queen
Mrs Thatcher is the Prime Minister

Ronald Reagan is the President of the United States
Four million people are unemployed
Ehiopia has a famine
South Africa has apartheid
Cruise missiles can kill a million people
Aids can kill everybody

If Social Services still think you're barking, barricade all doors and windows and get Ruth to come round in her uniform.

Kim.

THURSDAY.

Dear Nan,

I have just had a letter from the warden of St Agnes asking for my qualifications as a car mechanic! I have sent off my night school diploma and written to Scotch for a reference. I also enclosed a copy of my Driving Licence in case they need someone experienced to drive it (I am not very experienced at driving but I *am* very experienced with Scotch's motors. They usually have no brakes or clutch.)

They can pay wages for at least six months! They have got money from the government as it is election year.

Keep your fingers crossed,

Kim.

TUESDAY.

Dear Scotch,

How is the slimming going? My mother's friend Wendy Float had a cot death and she has never got over it though she has had nine other kids. She says you're doing a great thing, so I hope you are down to twelve stone! Scotch . . . I wonder if you'd have a word with the warden about me minding the Community Bus? I know we did not always see eye to eye (unless you picked me up by my earrings Ha! Ha!) and I *am* sorry about Tara's Porsche, I honestly thought it *was* only worth £500, but I for one certainly learned a lot whilst working at your yard. I hope now you have become a Christian you will let bygones be bygones and give me a good reference.

All the best to Tara and Cheyenne. (It's marvellous Cheyenne's learned the Rhumba now he's got the new foot.)

Be seeing you.

I hope.

Kim.

Geology Exhibition

TUESDAY.

Dear Ruth,

Thanks a lot for persuading the social services to wait 'til I hear about the job. I knew Nan would get her facts wrong, the only paper she reads is 'The Sun'. Mam is not very happy about me leaving. She says I have only just got there. I pointed out to her that six weeks may not seem long to her but it is a lifetime to someone with nothing to do. I tried to get Tracey to come and see an all-girl Acapella group who did a gig at the Astor, but she said anything with all girls was bound to be boring and anyway she had to hold Nigel's spare Rugby shirt while he practised Five-a-side. I have been to the museum three times and the art gallery four. They are full of pictures of men and machines. I've seen Rambo, The Killing Fields, Top Gun and Bambi. Bambi was dead upsetting. I've cleared the attic and re-painted my bedroom purple.

Mam insists on paying me for odd jobs. She says it's such a treat to have money of her own. She used to have to beg me dad for money for anything special. Like say food. Now we have treats all the time. On Saturday we went to a Soak and Sauna session in the new Health Club. We lay about reading magazines and eating Japanese food. She can be dead nice when she isn't trying to be my mother.

Kim.

The Warden,
St Agnes Community Centre.

MONDAY.

Dear Mrs Bhatachariya,

Thank you very much for the kind offer of a job as maintenance mechanic and driver of the community bus. I am glad Mr Salmon gave me such a glowing report. It's funny as he always used to say I didn't know a shaft rod from a big end.

I am very pleased to accept and will arrive to collect the bus from the scrap yard at nine o'clock sharp next Monday morning.

Yours sincerely,
Kim Kirby.

MONDAY.

Dear Nan,

I got the job! I can't wait to start! Marcus has got a client in London who can supply new parts for the engine. He always gets Marcus' cars at trade for tip offs on property prices. I am going to paint the bus a nice bright colour so it will always be a contrast with the graffiti and as soon as it is on the road we will have an Easter trip.

Mam has come round to the idea, now I have worked out how fast you can get to London in a BMW. Faster than a train judging by the timetable I am looking at. I am bringing a new cardigan for you from Mam, also jam, pickles, sheets, cake, a cat box and all Dusty's toys.

Am arriving on the three forty-five on Wednesday.

Love,
Kim.

MONDAY.

Dear Ruth,

I'm glad you've been able to put your training to use. Lucky it was you who was cooking the chops when the frying pan went up in flames.

I see that one of a fire fighter's duties is to 'render humanitarian service', so can you meet me off the train at three forty-five on Wednesday? I've got enough bags of stuff to start a Jumble sale and Nan isn't fit enough to help me carry it. You know she gets 'agitato' if she has to cross the Thames. Please come in your uniform . . . I don't suppose you could manage an engine? I've always wanted to be given a Fireman's Lift.

Looking forward to everything!

All the best,
Kim.

62 Prison View,
Borough of Lambeth,
London

WEDNESDAY.

Dear Mam, . . .

A selection of humour titles available in
paperback from Grafton Books

John Grant
The Depths of Cricket   £2.95 ☐

Sam Llewellyn
Yacky Dar Moy Bewty   £2.50 ☐

Neil Martin
A Devastatingly Brilliant Exposé of Almost Everything   £2.50 ☐

Gyles Brandreth
Great Sexual Disasters (illustrated)   £3.50 ☐

N Sayers and C Viney
The Bad News Zodiac   £1.95 ☐
The Bad News Horrorscope   £2.50 ☐

Ellis Weiner
National Lampoon's Doon   £2.50 ☐

To order direct from the publisher just tick the titles you want
and fill in the order form.   **GF2481**

All these books are available at your local bookshop or newsagent, or can be ordered direct from the publisher.

To order direct from the publishers just tick the titles you want and fill in the form below.

Name _____

Address _____

Send to:
Grafton Cash Sales
PO Box 11, Falmouth, Cornwall TR10 9EN.

Please enclose remittance to the value of the cover price plus:

UK 60p for the first book, 25p for the second book plus 15p per copy for each additional book ordered to a maximum charge of £1.90.

BFPO 60p for the first book, 25p for the second book plus 15p per copy for the next 7 books, thereafter 9p per book.

Overseas including Eire £1.25 for the first book, 75p for second book and 28p for each additional book.

Grafton Books reserve the right to show new retail prices on covers, which may differ from those previously advertised in the text or elsewhere.